They continued to
in the brilliant su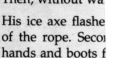

Then, without wa

His ice axe flashe
of the rope. Secol
hands and boots f
failing every time to get a grip. Gerry was dragged
down with him, also trying to get some kind of hold,
but Massey's bulk made it impossible. Then David
felt the deadly sharp pull of the rope. For a lunatic
moment he thought he might be able to support their
combined weight, but with whiplash cruelty he was
jerked off the ice and began to roll painfully from
ridge to ridge. Above him, the bland blue emptiness
of the sky mocked their audacious attempts at even
presuming to battle the Antarctic.

The fall seemed to go on for ever, and time after
time David glimpsed the sombre valley below with
its monolith rocks that now looked like tombstones.
He hit his head on an ice ridge, grazing his wrist on
another. This is it, he thought. This is the end of it
all . . .

**Also by Anthony Masters
and published by
Bantam Books:**

HELL ON EARTH

WHITE OUT

ANTHONY MASTERS

BANTAM BOOKS

ORONTO · NEW YORK · LONDON · SYDNEY · AUCKLAND

WHITE OUT

A BANTAM BOOK: 0 553 40802 X

First publication in Great Britain

PRINTING HISTORY
Bantam edition published 1994

Copyright © 1994 by Anthony Masters

Set in 11/14pt Linotype Palatino by Phoenix Typesetting,
Ilkley, West Yorkshire.

Bantam Books are published by Transworld Publishers Ltd,
61–63 Uxbridge Road, Ealing, London W5 5SA,
in Australia by Transworld Publishers (Australia) Pty Ltd,
15–25 Helles Avenue, Moorebank, NSW 2170,
and in New Zealand by Transworld Publishers (NZ) Ltd,
3 William Pickering Drive, Albany, Auckland.

Made and printed in Great Britain by
Cox & Wyman Ltd, Reading, Berks.

To Captain Nick Barker, ex-Captain of the *Endurance*, the Falklands guardship, who loves and understands the Antarctic wilderness, and whom I am fortunate enough to count as a good friend.

Also to Tom and Jemima, with love.

Peter Bishop knew that he couldn't hang on to the icy rock of the crevasse any longer. He had no idea what had happened below. Massey, who had been above him belaying, had disappeared as completely as Adam. So had the rope – except for the useless end around his waist. What could possibly have happened? How could the rope have broken? His two companions had totally vanished – been obliterated as if they had never existed. He had been calling out for a long time now and knew his strength was running out.

With the rope severed, he had no chance of going up or down. He was stuck with a hand-hold that wouldn't last much longer. Could he brace himself across the crevasse? He didn't think so, and if he tried and failed he would fall immediately. Not that he wasn't going to do that anyway. He stared at the green seam and the fortune it offered, but his triumph at the discovery had gone sour. He was going to die. Perhaps the others were already dead. No doubt the rumours of illegal interest were true, but he could never have imagined for one moment that they would go this far.

Peter thought of his son David who he had badly neglected for so long. He had been making mental resolutions not to allow the situation to continue – to be a real father to him at last. But now this was not to be. Risking everything, he released a hand and scratched on the ice face with his knife:

DAVID. I LOVE YOU. DAD.

He had only just finished the scrawl when his desperate grip on the rock gave way. As Peter plunged down the crevasse he was sure that he saw a skua bird at the top, blotting out the sun.

1

David had a recurring dream about the crevasse,
seeing his father falling down the narrow crack in
the ice, always falling, never finding the bottom
of the long, dark fissure. He saw the crevasse as
a white streak with blackened sides, his father a
tiny toy man, tumbling over and over, calling his
name. He stood at the top, watching him plummet,
helpless, terrified, the desperate call drumming in
his ears: 'David! David!'

He would wake sweating in the small stuffy
cabin of the *Patriot*, sitting up against the bulkhead,
staring down into the sheets, still seeing his father
falling.

On the fifth night of the dream there was a knock
on the door. Slowly the horror dropped away.

'Who is it?'

'Gerry.'

'Come in.' David was relieved to hear his
friend's voice, and when Gerry pushed open
the heavy varnished door he was even more
reassured by the boy's gawky frame and tousled
appearance. He was over two metres, a startled

crane. Predictably, Gerry banged his head on the lintel.

'You always do that,' David said.

'I know.'

Gerry was clumsy when he moved about the *Patriot*, the Royal Navy ice-breaker that was ploughing its way through heavy seas towards the shifting pack ice that surrounded Antarctica. Small, cramped areas were not his environment. Gerry was a long-distance runner and it was in the wide-open spaces that his tall, skinny body really came into its own, running with grace and speed amongst the wildlife that he so loved to study in his gentle, obstinate, conscientious way.

'What's up?' Gerry asked.

'Had a bad dream.'

'Again?'

'Fifth night running.'

'The crevasse?' asked Gerry tentatively.

'What else?'

Gerry's father, Adam Preston, and David's, Peter Bishop, had been missing for nearly a year in Antarctica and both boys had accepted that there was now no hope of finding them alive. Their fathers had been on a geological survey which mimicked Shackleton's first expedition, and they had also hoped to discover a new and important mineral that would revolutionize the microchip. Both were primarily scientists, and although they had been on arduous and potentially dangerous expeditions before, this was the one they hadn't returned from and Gerry and David, in their separate ways, were still grieving.

'You watched him?'

'All the way down.' David suddenly gave a half-sob. He tried to pull himself together and failed.

'We're getting closer. Don't you think it'll be better when we're at the base? We'll be nearer them.'

'Maybe.' David was not sure that he should have come after all. The long voyage had a special purpose – to create a memorial to the heroism of Adam Preston and Peter Bishop – and Gerry and David had run an obsessive and single-minded campaign to join the *Patriot* – and Tom Massey, the leader of their fathers' ill-fated expedition, who was someone they respected as much as the memory of their fathers. At first Massey had been very much against their involvement. He had been completely broken by the tragedy, blaming himself for what had happened although he had been completely cleared by the inquiry. Both Gerry and David realized that he saw his return to the Antarctic as an act of homage – one that he wished to undertake alone.

Geographica Magazine, who were financing the memorial, had insisted that Massey take both of them so that a story could be built around the sons of such famous fathers. Not only was he to take Gerry and David, but he was to photograph the expedition. Faced with such an ultimatum, Massey had agreed. A rough cairn was to be built by the boys and later this was to be made into something more permanent by staff from one of the Antarctic bases. He had also decided to take a young trainee from his adventure centre in Wales. YOUTH EXPEDITION TO THE ANTARCTIC the headlines had run. SONS TO RETRACE STEPS OF DEAD FATHERS. David still felt bitter that his mother had refused to come too. Peggy Preston had had a breakdown at the news of her husband's disappearance and was still in hospital, but David suspected that his own mother hadn't cared at all. Sandra Bishop had left his father for another man some years ago and he and his father had rarely seen her.

'Better get up. It's breakfast in ten minutes,' said Gerry.

'OK. What's wrong with Steve? He seems to be pretty down, doesn't he? I wish Tom hadn't brought him along now – he's so miserable all the time.'

'He's just a loser, isn't he?' Gerry had very firm ideas about life. If you flipped, you were a loser; if you stayed calm and thought your way through, you were a winner. It was a simple philosophy which David often objected to, particularly as Gerry frequently seemed to be all too irritatingly right in his judgements.

'Come on.' Even now he was implying that David was lazing in bed. 'I'm going for a run – see you in the canteen.'

Feeling as exhausted as he had the previous night, David stumbled out of his bunk, the dream still vividly replaying itself in his mind. He was much less confident than Gerry, and although he had grown to like him on the voyage far more than he had ever thought he would, when they had first met he had dismissed him as an eccentric boffin. David was a joiner; he liked to lose himself in a crowd and tended to be a follower rather than a leader. Since his mother had walked out, he had lived with his aunt, but his father had been remote and often absent throughout his life – so much so that he felt he had hardly known him. He partly yearned for him, partly hero-worshipped him. His father had never been quite real, although his disappearance had traumatized David, making him even more insecure than he had been before. As a result he had transferred much of the hero-worship he had felt for his remote father to Tom Massey, who was very much a household name, not just in England but all over the world. He had led many

13

expeditions both in the Arctic and Antarctic and had been involved some years ago in the heroic rescue of a crashed helicopter crew near the Pole. He had been in hospital for months afterwards with severe frostbite and a mental breakdown that had put him out of action for a much longer period of time. David remembered his father telling him that Massey should have been better looked after by the government rather than being allowed to go bankrupt after his illness. They had stayed with him several times in Wales since then and found him fully recovered, remarkably optimistic and raring to go on new adventures as he built up his outdoor-pursuits centre to recoup his financial losses.

'Bastard!' The word rang out suddenly in the companionway outside his cabin door. 'You bastard!'

David recognized the voice; it belonged to Steve Beck, the young and mercurial trainee adventure leader Massey had brought along. Steve came from Liverpool, a succession of children's homes, assessment centre, youth custody and more recently a placement at Massey's outdoor-pursuits centre in Wales. For years he had been a young criminal and was still unsure of his new role. He was both unstable and aggressive and seemed to have a very edgy relationship with Tom which had deteriorated during the long voyage. David couldn't think why, for Massey was tolerant and understanding, but at the same time David sneakingly felt sorry for Steve, for he knew what it was like to feel unsafe all the time. The difference between them was that David hid in a crowd and Steve stood out in one. Now it looked as if he was either in trouble, or was making trouble, again.

There came a thud and a cry of pain. David quickly opened his cabin door.

Tom Massey was lying in the companionway on his back, his big handsome head with its dark thatch of bushy hair upturned to his attacker. There was blood on his forehead and a gash on his cheek. Steve Beck stood over him, a large spanner in his hand and hatred in his pale blue eyes. He was short, squat, and the muscles in his bare white arms stood out like whipcords.

'I'll kill you.'

'Steve – for God's sake.'

'You try and stop me – I know what you're going to do.'

Massey started to struggle up. 'Back off.'

Steve ran at him, but Massey hooked his legs round the boy's ankle, bringing him crashing down. With considerable speed and agility, he rolled over on top of Steve, wresting the spanner from his grip. Then he sat astride him, pressing his knees into Steve's shoulders, talking fast, trying to calm Steve as he kicked and threshed. As he did so, the blood ran down Massey's face.

'Knock it off, Steve.'

'Bastard!'

'Knock it off – or I'll get the Captain to bang you up.'

The Second Officer, Jamie Fogg, hurried down the passage. He was an impatient man, clearly unhappy at the number of civilians *Geographica* had managed to saddle him with. And here they were, causing the trouble he had expected.

'What the hell's going on?' he demanded, picking up the spanner and holding it aloft.

Massey got off Steve, who scrambled to his feet. They both stood panting, looking acutely uncomfortable, aware now of David's silent presence.

'Nothing. Everything's under control.'

'Looks like it, doesn't it?'

'A bit of a problem. Now sorted out.'

Fogg ignored Massey. 'I'm not having this kind of thing going on.'

'It was a misunderstanding,' returned Massey.

'Misunderstanding? What do you think this ship is? A floating psychiatric unit? I've had more than enough of Beck, Mr Massey. He's a social experiment gone wrong – an accident waiting to happen – and I want him confined to his cabin until we reach Hayden Sound. So, if you'll report to the sick bay and get yourself fixed up, I'll take Beck to Captain Devon. Perhaps you'll join us in his cabin when you're ready.' There was a built-in sneer to Fogg's voice. Quite obviously he regarded Massey as an idealist.

Steve no longer seemed tough and truculent. Instead, he looked cowed and sulky – more like a little kid than anything else, thought David, despite the fact that Steve was built like an all-in wrestler.

'And you're just here for the blood, are you?' asked Fogg, wheeling round on David.

'I heard—'

'Sounds of a struggle outside your cabin? Well – it's over and you can start minding your own business, young man.' Fogg looked at his watch. 'It's time for your breakfast. Go and get it.'

'Knock it back,' commanded Gerry, fresh from his run and looking obscenely healthy.

David toyed with flaccid bacon and a flabby-looking poached egg. They seemed to specialize in under-cooking on the *Patriot*. Gerry and David were sitting alone at one end of the mess table, the crew huddled together at the other, talking ship's gossip in a desultory, grumbling sort of way. They had been roughly friendly to David and Gerry throughout the voyage, respectful to the memory of their fathers but clearly also regarding them as

17

an alien presence. They respected Tom Massey as a celebrity, an adventure leader and explorer, but the boys often found themselves out on a limb, grateful when occasionally drawn in.

'What's the rush?' asked David irritably.

'There's a berg coming up on the starboard bow. It's magnificent.' In January it was summer in Antarctica, and in a few days time they would be amongst the pack ice. Right now an encounter with their first iceberg should have been enthralling, but David was too concerned at what had happened between Steve and Tom to register what Gerry was saying.

'There's been more trouble with Steve,' David told him.

'Again?' Gerry was cynical.

'He attacked Massey. I think he hates him. I always reckoned that,' said David. 'But I can't think why.'

'It's only because he sees him as his gaoler.' Gerry had always had this theory.

'He's the bloke who's given him a chance.' David had a higher opinion of Steve than Gerry, which wasn't saying much as Gerry just regarded him as a loser. He had no time for Massey's do-gooding.

'That's not the way Steve looks at it,' said Gerry, irritating David yet again.

'Tom Massey's never got over losing our dads,' David persisted doggedly.

'He only just survived himself,' said Gerry. 'I'm not criticizing him over that, and you know I'm not. He's just a bit of a romantic when it comes to trash like Steve. Every time I've been down to Wales, I've always been impressed by Massey's integrity – his honesty. He's just fooling himself over this guy.'

'Even so —' David returned gloomily to his rapidly congealing breakfast. Gerry was hardly the most tolerant person he had met, but he also knew how worried Gerry was about his mother's mental condition. David sighed inwardly. Surely it was better to have a mother with a breakdown than no mother at all.

But when they both came out on deck, Gerry and David were transfixed. The iceberg was incredible in its translucent splendour. It was square-shaped, with dead white sides, and there were other bergs slowly coming up with lanes of blue-black water in between. The utter stillness was uncanny and the peaks flashed silver in the rays of the morning sun. A couple of snow petrels were perched on the lower edges of the glistening berg which had been weathered into fantastical shapes like a topiary garden on another planet. David had the impression of beginning a voyage through an unpopulated white city bisected by dark canals, while Gerry, ever down to earth, said, 'I'd love to get out on one of those. I wonder if we'll have the chance.'

Every now and then the silence was broken by a cracking sound as tonnes of ice and snow fell from the bergs, disturbed by the threshing of the *Patriot*'s screw.

'We'll be in the pack ice soon.' Gerry was excited, but David suddenly thought of his dad watching the same majestic monoliths, as that ill-fated expedition's small, partially decked whaler must also have edged past the bergs in the wake of Shackleton, the great Antarctic explorer.

Gerry gazed at the green and blue hues in the ice as the *Patriot* slipped past. 'Massey's never really talked about our dads' expedition, has he?' he said suddenly. 'Except to say that his breath froze and you had to go for a pee inside your pants. Just little details – nothing about what they really *did*. And we're only covering a fraction of the ground.'

'Massey hasn't talked to the Press and he's not going to write a book. He told me he wasn't. I guess he can't bear to think of it all because he could have made a bomb and he certainly needed the money. I'm sure it was a terrible blow to him. I mean – he's led loads of expeditions here *and* in the Arctic, and nothing ever went wrong that he couldn't handle.'

'Maybe he's still in shock,' observed Gerry, still staring out at the bergs.

'Do *you* think someone will find their bodies one day?'

'Unlikely. But I'd like them to be buried somewhere, with a cross and all that, wouldn't you?' Gerry sounded brisk – as if he wanted that part of life tidied up. 'But we'll get close to them on this expedition – experience just a bit of what they went through. I'd like to feel Dad. Feel him near me, I mean.' Gerry's voice shook, and David glanced at him in embarrassed surprise. This was the first time on the voyage that he had shown his feelings.

With relief, David saw Tom Massey walking down the deck towards them, long-legged, athletic, relaxed, with his black bush of a beard that matched his hair. His smile was warm and embracing and the only sign of the injury Steve had given him was a piece of sticking plaster on his cheek.

'Well?'

'It's magnificent,' said Gerry, and David mumbled agreement.

'Mr Massey, I've been—'

'How many times have I got to ask you to call me Tom? You've stayed with me in Wales – it's not as if we're strangers.'

'Tom – I've been thinking—' Gerry stuttered slightly and then recovered himself. 'What are the chances of finding their bodies?'

'Impossible.' Massey was adamant. 'I'm sorry.'

'It doesn't matter,' said David, although it did. As he spoke he felt a wave of annoyance with himself. Why did he always want to avoid upsetting people? Why couldn't he be more of an individualist?

'I'm feeling closer to them out here,' Gerry was saying.

'Good. I feel the same,' replied Massey, slightly haltingly.

'But not close enough,' said Gerry. 'I know we're retracing some of their steps, but – can we see the crevasse where they died? It was close to Rothera Base, wasn't it?'

Massey nodded. 'I'm not sure if I can find it again. I've tried to put it out of my mind, as you can imagine. But I'll try. As you know *Geographica* want the story to be centred on you, following the final leg of your fathers' journey. So perhaps we'll strike lucky.' His voice was hollow.

David was glad Gerry had been so forthright. If they found the crevasse then the dream might go away. He would also feel spiritually closer to a father he had idealized but who had always been a stranger. Gerry had known his father so much better – they had even been friends – and David was very jealous.

'Are you sure you're both able to trust me on this expedition? I know it's only a couple of days hard walking, but—' The question came as a surprise for they had not for one moment doubted his capability, nor had they wondered about Massey's personal confidence. He seemed invincible and, apart from his apparent belief in Steve, they knew his experience and judgement were absolutely sound.

Neither Gerry nor David could think of a reply. They hadn't expected such a question, and didn't know how to deal with it.

'After all—' Massey continued. 'I lost your fathers.' He was looking away from them, gazing out at the bergs.

'I've read about those crevasses – there's no warning,' said Gerry. 'And what about snow blindness?' He came to an abrupt halt, knowing he sounded hopelessly naive.

But Massey seemed to want to press home his self-criticism, and David wondered if Steve's extraordinary attack on him had shaken him up more than they realized. 'I'm an experienced leader, after all. Maybe I was careless.'

'We don't think so.' David was quick to support him.

'What brought all that on this morning?' asked Gerry cautiously, and David guessed that he had deliberately changed the subject. They had already been wondering what on earth Steve would be like on the trek. It might only be for two days, but if

Steve was going to behave as he had on board, they were all in for big trouble.

'He'd been drinking.' Massey seemed to tense up for a second and then shrugged. 'Managed to buy some whisky from the chef. He's found it hard, doing nothing but thinking and feeling an outsider. You're both balanced. Steve isn't. He's had the hell of a hard life. We had an argument over the booze and I said I wasn't having any more of it.' Massey glanced at Gerry. 'You think that's a sob story, do you? What's your opinion of him?'

'He seems a bit of a bullshitter.'

'He is. But he didn't have much of a chance to be anything else. I've had Steves before, but nobody as volatile as him.'

'But is he going to calm down?' asked David. 'What will he be like once we're out there?'

'He'll be fine,' said Massey firmly.

He sounded confident but both David and Gerry still had their doubts.

2

During the next twenty-four hours, the *Patriot* steamed into the pack ice. At first, Gerry and David could only make out a white glare on the horizon, but gradually they reached the broken mass. Captain Devon had told them the *Patriot* could manoeuvre freely in a heavy pack of more than five metres thick, and now her powerful engines were roaring as her sloping bow allowed the ship to ride up and then smash through the ice, her heavily reinforced hulls and kneeling tanks helping her to roll from side to side, freeing herself as she did so. Because of the amount of space taken up by her huge engines, there was very little room for cargo, so the *Patriot*'s main function was to break up channels for cargo ships to pass through. Shackleton's *Endurance* had been crushed by the pack ice in Weddell Sea in 1915, but since the large-scale exploration of the Antarctic since the Second World War, base stations required constant relief and there was a considerable flow of large bulk cargo.

Although David and Gerry had to perform some

duties on the *Patriot*, they also had considerable free time and they spent hours watching the ship crush the ice. The cold was intense and the chill factor rapidly increased with the slightest breath of wind. Visibility was good and David had the impression that he could see for miles, although he had no idea which was floating ice and which was the landmass. Also, he had no idea how far anything was for the distances were extremely deceptive.

Earlier, Massey had told them that the biggest problem in the Antarctic was 'white out'. 'It's really dangerous,' he had impressed on them. 'That's what happened to us – when your dads were lost. Despite the clarity of the air, there is no contrast so you don't have any real idea of the rise and fall of the landscape. You can easily fall over an ice cliff or stumble into a crevasse, just because you can't see them. In theory that sounds absurd, but just you wait until you've been out there in the thick of it.'

At about 6 p.m., the pack ice seemed to lessen and by half-past seven, Gerry and David could see open water.

'This is it. We'll get kitted up tomorrow and start the journey.' Massey leant over the bow, looking ahead. 'That'll be Hayden Sound coming up.' His fingers rapped a little tattoo on the railing.

He suddenly seems to have got very nervous,

thought David and wondered if Gerry had noticed. Maybe it was just the thought of taking Steve with them that had got him strung up, or were the real demons the memories of what had happened last time he had been in the Antarctic? David suddenly realized that this was going to be as much of a test for Massey as it was going to be for them. He wished he had thought of that before.

Steve Beck didn't seem to have calmed down at all, and as Gerry and David turned in for the night they could hear him bashing on his cabin door, yelling abuse and calling for Massey. Then Captain Devon arrived in person and his admonishing voice seemed to quieten Steve at last.

'It's going to be tough out there.'

David tried to joke as he sat on Gerry's bed, reluctant to go to his own cabin, knowing that the crevasse dream was likely to return to him. 'We're going into the white hell, so it's all chaps on the alert.'

'You don't sound that keen.' Gerry gave him a long hard look. He could be perceptive at times. 'We don't have to go out there.'

'I'm only joking.'

'Sure?'

'Yes, I'm sure. The expedition's going to help – and maybe the dream will disappear after we've done the trek.'

'Do you know something? I sometimes can't remember what my dad looked like.' Gerry turned away from him. 'Maybe I'll see him again if we go – like you'll forget your dream. I really concentrate but I still can't see his face.'

David sensed that Gerry was crying now, but he knew better than to try and comfort him. The irony was that he hadn't always been able to remember his own father's face – even when he had been alive. But then he had been so remote, making so few trips home. Of course, it hadn't really been his home – just a stop-over.

'I'll be getting to bed then.'

'Good-night.' Gerry managed to steady his voice, but only just.

David didn't sleep for a long time because he kept thinking about his father. Peter Bishop had been a geologist all his working life, specializing in researching mineral belts around the world and trying to discover whether they held potential. Until David's mother had left home just before his eighth birthday, they had been a happy and united family, despite his father's travels. Peter had always been remote, locked away in his threatening outside world, but nevertheless David could remember them playing football on the beach, going for a run each morning when his father was at home, and playing chess on winter evenings. Once, when his swimming had not been strong enough for a particularly rough sea, his father had saved him, pulling him on his back through lashing waves. They had lain together on the beach exhausted. But after that, David had seen his father less and less. Perhaps his mother had felt she was married to a stranger too, for a few months later she left home for someone else. His aunt had taken him to live with her and his father rarely visited them. Auntie Zoe was a widow who had had no children, but she was warm and sensitive and didn't spoil him rotten. He had grown to love her, but he still yearned after the father he barely knew.

Gradually David drifted off to sleep, still wondering if going on to the mainland and experiencing at least some of the conditions his father had faced would bring him any closer. It was an intriguing idea.

The dream came back towards morning when David was sleeping more lightly, and it was different and even more disturbing. This time, he was lying on his stomach on shifting snow, his hands round his father's wrists. Somehow Peter Bishop had managed to pull himself up the crevasse, but now, with just centimetres to go, his strength was exhausted. Gripping his father's wrists tightly, David knew that he alone could rescue his father, just as his father had rescued him from the sea. But he also knew that his own strength was running out.

'Who are you?' he kept asking. 'Who are you?' But his father only gave him an impatient shake of the head. 'I can't pull you up until I know who you are,' David insisted, realizing his grip was weakening. His father refused to reply, and finally he slid away from David's failing grasp and plunged back into the crevasse, twisting and turning as he fell. When David awoke, sweating and desperate, he was still pleading, 'I must know who you are. I can't pull you up – not until I know who you are.'

Next morning after breakfast, David and Gerry met up with Tom Massey and a silent, subdued Steve in one of the *Patriot's* equipment stores.

Massey was in a brisk and authoritative mood, but he managed to be reassuring as well. 'On a fine summer's day out here in the Antarctic you can sunbathe as if it's a ski resort, but one breath of wind will send you running for cover. It's the sharpest chill you'll ever experience, as painful as a knife wound, and if you're not adequately dressed that knife will keep twisting.'

Gerry shuddered; even to his practical soul, Massey's description was intimidating.

'It's called the wind-chill factor and it gives de-signers of polar clothing a nasty headache,' Massey admitted. 'Wind-chill can attack any exposed part of the body and give you frostbite, which is the equivalent of a burn. Protective skin is killed off and the damaged area puffs up like a balloon. Unless the circulation can be restored, gangrene will set in. I've lost two toes like that. If the core of the body is really chilled,' he paused reflectively, 'you start falling into a state of lethargy. Soon after that you'll die.'

There was a short, anxious silence, and then he continued. 'After a day's walking and climbing you'll be exhausted. When you get into your sleeping bag, all your clothing which was originally full of frozen sweat gets warmed through, and you'll feel decidedly damp. There's no possibility of ever getting anything dried, or of even getting any clothes off, except socks, which have to be changed night and day to avoid getting frostbite. I'm not trying to wind you up, just warning you that it's a hostile wilderness out there – probably the most hostile place you'd find anywhere in the world.' He pulled out a pile of clothes from a locker. 'The modern polar suit should insulate the body from the cold, be easy to wear and be light-weight and comfortable.' He laughed. 'That's what the manufacturers say, and they're dead right.'

Gerry winced at the word 'dead' and Steve grinned. He tried to wipe it away immediately but Gerry glanced at him angrily.

'This is the latest fashion choice.' Massey laughed again hopefully, trying to cover up his verbal blunder with a neat joke.

No-one responded.

'Next to the skin a two-piece undershirt and long-johns,' continued Massey rather mechanically. 'All these are made of cotton or wool which create air pockets so the fabric can trap warm air and provide insulation. Over this you've got windproof trousers and a jacket made of cotton or nylon. There's a hood to the jacket and underneath that you wear a cap. On your hands you'll have these outsize mittens with leather palms, and on your feet you'll have thermal boots which are completely waterproof. They feel damp because sweat accumulates in the boot. Actually, it takes quite a bit of getting used to, walking about with wet feet, but since the boots are so well insulated no heat is lost at all. All you have to do each day is to remember to dry your socks. I can't emphasize that too much. Now – the total weight of this polar suit is only about seven kilograms, as against the twenty-kilogram clothing worn by the likes of Shackleton and Scott. Any questions?'

'What are we going to sleep in? Tents?' asked Gerry.

'There's a wooden hut for the first night, and after that there'll be a lightweight tent that should take us all comfortably.'

'And food?' asked David all too eagerly.

Massey smiled, glad to be back on an easier level. 'Fifty years ago there were two fates that could have overtaken a polar expedition: scurvy or slow starvation. Scurvy is caused by a lack of vitamin C and was one of the causes of Scott and his companions' deaths in 1912. But that's not a problem with modern freeze-dried foods, and we'll be taking some of those with us. They can be reconstituted in minutes simply by soaking in water.' He paused and then hurried on, suddenly looking uneasy. 'So those are the main practicalities. We'll have rucksacks, skis and snowboots – get those fitted later.' He turned to David. 'There was a poem your father used to quote at me, and before we came on this trip I looked it up and made a copy. Thought you might like to read it.' He smoothed out a piece of paper on the flat surface of an old trunk and they all leant over. 'It's only a section of a poem by Browning, but I know it struck a cord with Peter. In fact, he quoted it on our last night together.

'Fear death? – to feel the fog in my throat,
The mist in my face,
When the snows begin, and the blasts denote
I am nearing the place,
The power of the night, the press of the storm,
The post of the foe;

33

Where he stands, the Arch Fear in a visible form,
Yet the strong man must go;
For the journey is done and the summit attained.'

There was a long silence, broken in the end by Tom Massey. 'We'll be getting going in a couple of hours,' he said quietly, 'but I wanted to say something before we start. Your fathers were very brave men and I was privileged to be with them on that expedition. You know how desperately sorry I am about what happened. But I shall always remember them as the finest individuals I've ever met – or worked with.'

David was deeply moved and he could see that Gerry felt the same, but when he glanced at Steve he thought there was a slight smile on his lips. It vanished almost immediately, and later David wondered if his vivid imagination had got the better of him.

3

The sun was high in an ice-blue sky as Massey steered the Zenith rubber dinghy past the ice promontory towards the shore.

'The light's amazing,' said Steve, speaking rather awkwardly. 'You can see for miles.' Was he trying to be friendly? wondered Gerry. Attempting to reassure them that he was going to be 'all right' on the expedition? He hoped so.

'That's why it's so dangerous,' replied Massey. 'Don't forget what I said. Distances are completely deceptive. We *must* stay together when we kick off. No way does anyone go anywhere alone. I've got a radio and will be in touch with the wireless operator on the *Patriot* at all times.'

Gerry looked around wonderingly. He had never come across a place that was so primeval and his father's words echoed in his mind. 'You'll never appreciate the Antarctic until I take you there, Gerry. And one day I will.'

But he couldn't now and here Gerry was, on his own, with the man who had led the expedition which had accidentally killed the one person he had loved more than anyone else in the world. Yet Gerry had always had the utmost respect for Massey. Despite what had happened, nothing would shake that conviction.

The mountain range, with its overloaded snow shelves, streaking glaciers and crevasses, looked almost within reach, but was, in fact, some miles away. The beach was desolate, with grey shale and pebbles, and the hut, which was just below a rocky promontory, looked totally inadequate. Whalebones were scattered over the foreshore, and bits of iceberg littered the shallow waters. David immediately noticed a sharp, acrid smell.

'What's that?' he asked.

'Guano. Penguin shit. It stinks to high heaven. The rookery's just round the corner.'

Oil drums, crates and rusting, unidentifiable machinery were piled around the battered hut, and the hulk of an old whaler lay beside it.

'It's the end of the world,' said Steve.

'Or the beginning,' Gerry muttered.

Once they were out of the Zenith, Massey organized them into gathering firewood. Maybe he thinks we'll get used to the place if we carry out some mundane task, thought David, but he knew he never would. He remembered the poem that Massey had read out earlier – the poem his dad had liked so much – and felt deeply depressed. It seemed to set them even further apart.

'I'll get a fire going soon,' said Massey. 'Amazing what a difference a can of petrol can make.'

The air was dry, almost warm, but there was a darting breeze that blew from the sea and it made David shiver even with his protective clothing. Under the wickedly gleaming mountains there was moss and lichen covering some of the old snow and ice from last winter. The terrain looked as if it was lying in wait for him, and the only cheerful sight was the *Patriot* standing offshore and the distant buzz of a transistor radio on board. The ship looked peaceful, cosy – the only remnant of civilization left to them.

'Does it get dark?' asked David, staggering under what felt like his own weight in firewood.

'Don't you notice *anything*?' Massey was surprisingly irritable and Gerry wondered just how well he concealed his bad nerves. 'We've been steaming through this for days now.' Then he seemed to relent, but the warmth came back into his voice too quickly, as if it had been forced. 'At this time of year the sun goes down, but instead of night there's a kind of perpetual twilight. Useful if you've got a long way to go.'

After a backbreaking period of working on the sharply shelving pebbles, Massey said they had collected enough firewood and they went into the hut to clear the fireplace. The interior was a jumble of broken furniture. The snow had seeped through on one side of the roof, and there was a long, dark stain on the wall. The place was dismal, but once the fire had been lit and they discovered the chimney was in working order, the atmosphere seemed less bleak.

'I'm starving,' said David, whose mind had once again returned to the comfort of food.

Massey looked at his watch. 'Half-twelve. Let's get all the equipment in and we'll brew up.'

Much to David's frustration, stocking the hut with provisions, sleeping bags, a camping stove and a couple of kerosene lamps took another ten minutes, but eventually, after some hurried preparations, they sat down to a meal of baked beans, hot coffee and cold rice pudding from a tin. In the light of the crackling flames and with the forbidding landscape held at bay outside, the simple food tasted wonderful.

Steve seemed to have gone silent again and David knew they would have to reach him if he was to have a chance of feeling part of the group. Wasn't Massey taking a considerable risk in bringing him after all that had happened? For his part, and he was sure Gerry's, David resented having him along. He was a problem and he wasn't sure the situation would allow for problems.

'As you know, the *Patriot* will sail this afternoon and pick us up at Rothera Base, probably on Wednesday.' Massey's confident gaze swept them.

'We'll be in constant radio contact with her and they can call up a chopper if necessary, so don't worry. We're going to have an important experience – all four of us. The forecast isn't brilliant, so what we're going to do is to spend the night here and start out for Halley in the morning. The journey should take a couple of days. We'll spend the third night at the base and meet the *Patriot* the following morning. Everyone understand?'

'Is there anyone at the base?' asked Gerry.

'No, but it's fully equipped and there's an Argentine weather station a mile up the coast so we can contact them if we need to. But I don't anticipate that happening.'

'What sort of weather's coming up now?' asked Steve rather self-consciously.

'Wind and possibly a blizzard. You'll know when it comes.' Massey grinned. 'We'll bunk down in here. It should be clear by the morning. Why don't you two get more driftwood?' He nodded to Gerry and David. 'If you're quick you could take a look at the penguin colony round the corner. It's quite a sight as I remember it. But don't stay long. First hint of bad weather you come straight back here. Meanwhile, Steve and I will try to make this place more habitable.'

'Do you think he wanted us out of the way?' asked David as they trudged over the slippery pebbles that were covered with snow melt and ice.

'Why should he?' Gerry was abstracted, thinking about the penguins more than anything else.

'Maybe he wants to try and sort Steve out before we begin the expedition. Give him a pep talk.'

'He needs a boot up the arse,' said Gerry, brutal as ever.

As they stumbled on towards the black primeval cliffs, the sound began to assault their ears and the smell nearly asphyxiated them. Guano. Acrid and horribly potent. Then they rounded the corner and stopped dead, for the sight was bizarre and amazing. There were literally thousands of nesting penguins in a tightly packed rookery in what looked like a volcanic crater. Ash covered the floor of the ravine as well as banks of guano.

'What are those birds?' asked David. 'They look dodgy.'

'They're called skuas – and they are!' replied Gerry.

One of the birds flew in low from the sea to swoop on a runtish chick, tearing the struggling creature apart in seconds. It was a macabre and tragic sight, but no doubt a matter of routine to the beleaguered rookery.

'It's the males who incubate the eggs,' said Gerry with his usual ornithological authority. 'While he's sitting on the egg he fasts and the female hunts for food. And when the chick hatches it sits at the feet of either its father or its mother who both feed it with regurgitated fish or squid or krill. It can't go down to the sea and forage for itself until it's about six months old.'

'So the survival rate isn't high?' said David, watching the marauding skuas hovering in the sky.

'Slight over-population problem too,' said Gerry.

'I can't see how these male penguins can find their own nests.'

'Mistakes can be made, but not so many. I've read up on it.'

He would, David thought with affection.

'Each penguin that returns from the sea has memorized the pitch of its mate's voice, and each chick knows both its parents' voices. Amazing, isn't it? You'd like it – could lose yourself in the crowd here all right,' added Gerry, grinning at him.

'I thought you said they were all so perfectly identified,' retorted David.

They stood and watched for a while, ignored by the chick-rearing males and females covered in guano, and those who had just come back from the sea, fresh and smooth. Other members of the rookery floated on the boiling surf and, further out, David could see a few floating bodies.

'They seem to have so many enemies.'

'Skuas in the rookery; seals and orcas out at sea. Hazardous living.'

'What kind of penguins are these?'

'Chinstraps. Hard-working optimists. They breed, raise chicks, feed – and breed again. Only the strongest survive.'

David was fascinated by the activity, but repelled by the filthy conditions and the carnage. Suddenly he was reminded forcibly of the slums of Victorian London he had read about at school, with the skuas playing the role of Jack the Ripper. Then his thoughts turned back to his father. Had he stood here and watched this amazing society and come to similar conclusions? Suddenly David was seized with the overpowering urge to ask Gerry about *his* relationship with his own father – a subject he had hardly touched on as yet for fear of seeming too intrusive.

'You were close to your dad, weren't you?'

'When he was around,' said Gerry enigmatically, rather to David's surprise. Then he felt David's need. 'Yes, I was. He was like me – bit of an oddball. He only talked on the subjects that really grabbed him. Like penguins.' He chuckled. 'I tell you something though – that was the first time they'd been together for such a long time, that expedition—'

And the last, thought David with a dreadful

wrench. 'I bet they were really good mates.'

'I'm sure they were.'

They stood rather awkwardly, looking at each other, not knowing what else to say. Suddenly their thoughts were interrupted.

'Like Piccadilly Circus, isn't it?' They turned round to see Steve, short, brutish and somehow sardonic. He looked oddly at home in the rookery.

'Tom wants you back. He says the weather's changing.'

'We're only a couple of hundred metres away from the hut.' David looked up to see the sky was no longer bright but was becoming overcast with a leaden grey. 'What's coming. A blizzard?'

'Wind.'

'OK. Let's go,' said Gerry, ever respectful of the elements.

'Hang on.'

'What's up?'

'Want to talk to you.' Steve was hesitant.

'You said we had to get back,' reprimanded David.

'Five minutes won't make no difference.'

'Well?' Gerry and David looked at him curiously.

'You got to watch him.'

'Who?' asked Gerry sharply.

'Massey.'

'Why?'

'He's not what you think.' Steve looked round furtively and, for the first time, David wondered whether he was afraid.

'I don't get you,' said Gerry, deliberately obtuse, trying to draw him out.

'He's a bastard. And putting up a monument isn't what he's about.' His voice was low and sullen but there was a truculence too.

'What *is* he about then?' asked Gerry condescendingly, as if Steve had the lowest possible IQ.

'Making some loot. Foreign bloke phoned him in Wales. I listened in.'

'Well?' David felt angry that Steve should be putting Massey down in such an obviously fabricated way.

'Them minerals – the ones your dads were looking for. They're going to meet up, and Massey's going to authenticate their location. That's what he said. And this foreign bloke said that if he could, he'd get eighty thousand quid in cash.' Steve smiled.

He's just winding us up against Massey, thought David and a wave of anger swept over him. As if things weren't difficult enough. Now they'd got themselves a right shit-stirrer.

'He wouldn't talk about anything like that on a phone. Come on, pull the other one.'

Steve frowned. 'Course he would. The phone's a private one.'

'With an extension?'

'Yeah – in his own sitting-room. He lives alone, and I'm not meant to be in his house.'

'So why were you?' asked David.

'He'd been acting funny – jumping every time the phone rang and dashing off to answer it. Bag of nerves ever since he got back from here last year. Does a good cover-up though, doesn't he?' The malicious smile was back on his face.

'Look.' Gerry decided to try and set some kind of seal on the next few days. 'You shouldn't be implying things about him like that. You're only winding us up. We've got total trust in Massey and you'd better remember that. What's more, it's really essential for us all to get on together. If we don't, it could be really dangerous.'

'Yes,' David agreed, 'you can't make up things just because you've had a row with the guy.'

They were having to shout over the noise of the rookery and the conversation was becoming farcical.

'He's been threatening me. No-one does that. I got a temper, see, so that's why I went for him.'

'Threatening you with what?' asked Gerry.

'Said he'd get me back in court. That means I'd be banged up again.'

'Why should he do that?'

'Said I was always spying on him.'

'He's got a point,' said David.

'I wanted to know what he was up to. I mean, how long have you known the guy?' He was still looking back warily along the beach.

'Long enough. We've spent quite a lot of time with him.'

'So you think he's a good bloke, do you?' The mocking note in Steve's voice intensified.

'Of course,' said Gerry.

'That's what I thought you thought.' He grinned unpleasantly.

'What are you trying to say?' David shivered. It was definitely getting colder and far more overcast. Also, he could feel the first stirrings of a wind that cut like ice.

'I'm trying to say he's like two blokes.'

'Come *on.*' Gerry was impatient.

'One OK. The other – evil.'

Gerry laughed contemptuously.

'You got any evidence of this?' David tried for the last time to be logical.

'Plenty.' Steve sounded confident and there was a long tense pause.

The ice seemed to stir somewhere inside David now as he wondered just how paranoid Steve was.

'He's like one of them big birds,' he muttered.

'A skua?'

'Yes. Diving for the kill.'

'Bollocks.' Gerry looked at his watch. 'Come on – we should be getting back, or he really *will* kill us.'

'Why don't you take me seriously?' Steve's mood changed. Suddenly he was an animal again. His arms hung by his sides and his eyes glinted oddly. He looked primeval and slightly mad, just like the rookery – or the landscape – or the South Pole itself. 'Ever thought he might have killed your dads? Because they'd found the minerals? Eighty grand is a lot of money. Worth taking a risk for. I mean, maybe Massey was just waiting for the minerals to be found. That was his plan.'

'Why don't you piss off?' shouted David, glaring at Steve with loathing and contempt.

'Eh?'

'Piss off!'

'Don't you speak to me that way.'

'We'll report you to Massey. That was a rotten, rotten thing to say.' Gerry's voice trembled. He looked deeply shocked.

'Rotten! Rotten!' Steve mocked him.

Without thinking, his emotions at full flood now, David punched him hard in the chest, but the blow seemed to have no effect at all and Steve only grinned provocatively.

'I'm only trying to make you see that side of Massey – that evil side you won't recognize.'

'I'll bloody kill you,' yelled David.

'No you won't.'

'Why are you telling us all this crap?' asked Gerry, looking at Steve as if he was crazy.

'Thought you should know. You're a couple of Boy Scouts, aren't you? Who do you think Massey is? Baden Powell? I mean, he's not exactly Captain Scott, is he?'

'Why have you come here?' asked David in utter misery.

'To see justice done.' Steve gave them another mocking smile.

'You hate Massey, don't you?'

'He's a patronizing bastard.'

'He's kept you out of trouble,' observed Gerry.

'Not any more.'

'Why don't you admit the truth?' David was still pugnacious and Gerry looked at him in surprise.

'What truth?'

'You're just making it all up because you've got into trouble on the ship.'

'No way.' But Steve was on the defensive now.

Gerry took over. 'You wanted to put us against him by telling us this filthy lie about our dads.' David glanced at him and realized that Gerry was also boiling with a steely rage very like his own. 'So it's us you have to look out for – us you should be afraid of. Not Tom Massey. You're sick, Steve. You need treatment.'

'Shut up!' Steve looked hunted.

He's either desperately trying to be confident, thought Gerry, or has his back against the wall. He was sure that Steve was in the latter position a great deal.

'You're unhinged.' David joined in, his anger still growing.

Steve stared at him with considerable distaste and then switched his gaze to Gerry who was clenching and unclenching his fists. Pushing David aside with such force that he fell on to the stinking ash, he advanced on Gerry and hit him in the stomach. Gerry doubled up in pain and then also went down on the ash and guano.

Without thinking, David scrambled up and grabbed Steve's shirt, yanking him round. But before he could do anything else, a voice yelled, 'Stop that! Now!'

4

Steve turned towards Tom Massey who was clambering over the rocks. He looked cowed.

'What happened?' Massey strode commandingly over the ash while the penguins, oblivious of the human conflict, or perhaps only regarding it as an extension of their own battles, continued to screech.

The shouting match between Gerry and Steve had brought a row of small penguins around them. They seemed to hover admiringly.

'Let's get back to the hut and sort this out,' said Massey furiously. 'There's bad weather coming up and we can't afford to be caught unprepared – or behaving like a pack of squabbling kids.'

They stumbled over the rocks, Gerry still holding his stomach and Steve looking surprisingly ashamed.

David felt confused and miserable. Massey should never have brought Steve along. He was a total nutter, David thought angrily, and a dangerous one. Just wait till I tell Massey what Steve said, he thought. Everything was spoilt because Steve was here.

Back in the hut, with the sky becoming whiter and visibility noticeably shortening outside, Gerry said, 'Is this going to be a white-out?' Somehow, his desire to get Steve into further trouble seemed to have vanished.

'It may end that way, but it's a blizzard we're going to get in a moment. Listen to that wind.'

It was certainly mounting. The waves were growing bigger and little flurries of snow were already blowing off the rocks. The interior of the hut, less squalid now, seemed almost welcoming.

'What about the Zenith?' asked David.

'I pulled her right up behind a rock and lashed her down,' said Massey. 'She'll be fine. But *we're* not. You've only been here a short while and already you're at each other's throats.'

'Steve started it,' said David.

Massey sat down in front of the driftwood fire. 'This expedition – like all expeditions – is in the nature of an experiment in trying to live with each other. I don't want to know what happened—'

'Wait a minute!' said Gerry.

'I *said*, I don't want to know what happened. We've *got* to get on. If we don't then our lives will be in danger. I realize that last year's expedition ended in tragedy, but paradoxically we all got on really well. Right to the very end. But now our situation's different. Peter and Adam were experienced explorers as well as geologists; you three are raw recruits – raw as hell. It's even more essential to make a real effort. Got it?'

While the lecture continued, David glanced discreetly at Steve. He looked beaten and his eyes were dull and lifeless.

Massey continued. 'Steve's not an easy guy, as you can see, but in preparation for the expedition I put him through hell over the last two weeks back in Wales.'

'I almost drowned in that canoe,' Steve accused, but now he just sounded like a sulky child.

Gerry looked impatient but David almost felt sorry for him, despite all the hurtful lies he had told.

'I was pushed too far,' Steve grumbled. 'Got mixed up in that "dubbin your boots and climb Everest and you'll be a man my son" kind of bullshit.' Steve suddenly grinned disarmingly at them.

So he *is* intelligent, thought David with the same kind of shock that Gerry had felt earlier. *And* he's got a sense of humour.

But David was wondering what kind of game Steve was playing. He was sure that was what he was doing, but what on earth was his objective?

'With the weather closing in, we've really got to

look out for each other,' Massey insisted. 'We've *all* got our faults – including me – but we've got to bury them for as long as it takes. Right?'

All three nodded dutifully.

'We have to go forward. The *Patriot*'s on course for Rothera Base and she can't get back here that easily – there's a good deal of pack ice building up now. I've been in radio contact and I'll stay that way.'

'We're not yomping through a blizzard, are we?' asked Gerry.

'Don't worry – it'll blow itself out.'

'We've got complete faith in you,' said David loudly so that Steve would hear. Later, when they were safely back on the *Patriot*, he would tell Massey about the incredible things Steve had said, but right now he was all for unity and he was certain that Gerry felt the same.

Then, surprisingly, Steve apologized. 'I wound you up – wound you all up. I weren't right. I'm sorry.'

Massey clapped him on the shoulder before anyone else could say anything.

David and Gerry found Steve's admission completely out of character. Why had he caved in so quickly after his furious outburst and accusation, or was he *really* scared of Massey? And if so – why? There was something going on that wasn't quite right. Was it David's own misinterpretation?

Or— David felt exhausted by the permutations.

'OK, Steve, we accept that,' said Massey. 'But you'll have to change your attitude. We can't leave you here. You do realize that. The *Patriot* may not be able to put in for days and the chopper can't operate if conditions harden up.' Massey picked up his radio and stared gloomily at it. 'I can't put everyone's lives at risk. If there's the slightest potential for trouble—'

'It's all right.' Steve's voice was steady and re-assuring. 'After a couple of months of your torture chamber of an adventure centre I should be just fine for our little walk.'

'It's tougher than you think. We can only ski along the tops of the mountains. It's bloody hard trudging up and down in snowshoes.' Massey seemed to have lost his sense of humour.

'Yeah. I'll manage.' Steve yawned. 'Anything else to eat?'

Later, when Gerry and Tom Massey were outside making a last check on the Zenith, Gerry voiced his concern. 'Is he really up to it?'

'Physically, he's resilient and strong. It's just his emotions that are in tatters.'

'That'll make him unpredictable.'

'He's made his protest—'

'Some protest.'

'And got the hatred for me off his chest, I expect.

Steve is so wilfully independent that he can't take any help of any kind – specially from someone older than him.'

'You really think so?'

'I know him inside out.'

'Do you want to know what he said to us?'

'No, old son, I don't. I told you that before.'

Gerry knew he had to be satisfied. He wanted to stay on good terms with Massey, all too well aware of the physical demands they had to face. He wanted his respect – and would probably need some sympathy. Gerry was beginning to feel increasingly nervous about the expedition, particularly as the weather looked as if it was really closing in now.

'It's all right,' said Massey, sensing his anxiety. 'The wind hasn't got up as much as I thought it might, so we're not going to have to worry about a blizzard.'

And tomorrow?'

'Things can change quickly here, but I think we're going to be all right.'

'What happens if it gets bad while we're in the mountains?' asked Gerry warily.

'We'll bivvy down. I've got everything we need, including survival bags. But we're talking about a hike, not a major expedition. Once we get to Rothera Base – which is extremely well equipped – we can stay there for days if needs be.'

Gerry was much more level-headed and far less a prey to his emotions than David and consequently he was beginning to wonder if David understood Steve better than he did. They both shared fantasies: Steve with his hatred and indignation, David with his obsessive search for the truth about his father's last hours.

As he walked back to the hut, Gerry had the unsettling feeling that the elements were lying in wait, setting a trap for them all. The wind seemed to be in hiding, gently yet resolutely whistling round the rocks; the sea had a vicious curl and the sky was dark and leaden. Antarctica had them all under surveillance.

Once again, David couldn't sleep. Too much had happened and he now dreaded the expedition – largely because of Steve but partly because he was wondering if he was up to it himself. He had always been a rather nervous skier, not like Gerry who was an accomplished athlete, and he wondered if he was going to be a liability.

Towards the early hours of the morning he drifted off, temporarily released from the sound of the wind droning outside and the waves shifting the ice on the foreshore. It made a strange human groaning sound.

Minutes later – or so it seemed – David woke and sat up, thinking that someone had gone out, but when he looked round he thought he could see the others tightly wrapped in their sleeping bags. Then he saw the note tucked into the top of his own.

> *Dave,*
>
> > *You are the only guy who might believe me. Gerry has written me off and Massey is afraid. Afraid and dangerous. Don't show him this note. If you do, he'll kill me. He may do that anyway, but I'm watching my back and it's either him or me. Odds on it's me though.*
>
> > > > *Steve*

David lay back, his heart pounding. His first instinct was to wake Massey, show him the note and wait for another confrontation. But what could be gained by that? Maybe if Steve thought he had a friend, then he would behave more reasonably than if he felt he was surrounded by enemies.

But David knew he had to bear one thing in mind: Steve was definitely disturbed.

Now the wind was calling him, but it had a voice. His father's voice.

'David.'

He buried himself deeper into his bag. He mustn't answer the call. The wind was his enemy.

'David.'

Standing at the window he could only see caked

snow. Shivering in his long-johns, he paused, trying to shake himself awake but failing.

'David. I need help.'

He felt unutterably confused, but nevertheless stepped silently over the others and cautiously opened the door.

The wind was sharp, darting, but only in gusts.

He closed the door and peered out of the window again. Down by the sea, he could just make out a figure. Tall and monstrous. Primeval.

'I need help.' The voice rang in his mind. 'Help me! Help me, David.'

He opened the door again and went outside, feeling the full thrust of the freezing night.

The thing in the shallows was waiting for him.

Strong arms caught David round the waist and held on to him. He struggled and then woke fully. The thing was still there.

'Shush.'

'Who is it?'

'Steve.'

'Let go!'

'Not until you promise to come in. You was sleep-walking. I saw you go and followed.'

'OK.'

Steve released him and there was a dim roar from the shallows.

'What's that?'

'Elephant seal, I think. Big blubbery smelly thing.'

'How do you know?'

'Tom told me. Did you get my note?'

'Yeah.' David was cautious, placating.

'Not going to show it to him?'

'No,' he said, much against his better judgement.

'It's all true.'

'Look—' David paused. How *could* he reason with Steve? He was so unpredictable. So paranoid.

'You think I'm crazy, don't you? You watch my back tomorrow – and I'll watch yours.'

David sighed. He could spend ages telling Steve that Massey was someone who could be trusted. But what was the point? Steve would never listen.

'Do you often sleep-walk?' Massey and Gerry were sitting up in their sleeping bags, looking concerned.

David felt really ashamed. 'No.'

'Thanks, Steve.' Tom Massey gave him a rather sanctimonious look as if he was acknowledging the beginning of Steve's rehabilitation, as designed by himself.

'I thought I heard my dad's voice.' David tensed, waiting for them to laugh, but no-one did – not even Steve.

Massey struggled up and put his arm round

David's shoulders. 'I'll do anything to lay this ghost.' His use of words was clumsy and unfortunate, but he clearly meant well, although David was not sure that he wanted him to lay the ghost, for while his father still called to him there was hope. It was probably all as mad as Steve's paranoia, but much better than the grim reality of knowing his father was dead.

Massey glanced at his watch. 'We must turn in now – got to be up in a couple of hours.' He listened to the wind that was coming and going in unsettled gusts.

'It's playing with us,' muttered Gerry, and David's stomach gave a sharp little wrench. How strange it was that Gerry's thoughts were so close to his own now. Were they both becoming intuitive out here?

David burrowed into his sleeping bag, making sure that Steve's note was well down in his pocket. He mustn't leave it around – in fact, he should try and destroy it as soon as possible. Poor Steve, he thought, as he slid into the blessed relief of deep sleep. Steve was in a very bad way. But he needed a friend.

'You've got to get up.'

'Mm.'

'Up, Dave. *Now*.' Tom Massey was standing over

him, dark shadows under his eyes, already dressed in his polar suit and wearing snowshoes. 'We've got to move.'

'What's the weather like?' David mumbled.

'Much like last night. Unsettled. But we have to get on.' He paused and said reflectively, 'Funny – I've never known it hold off like this.'

'We'll camp tonight then?'

'And arrive at the base tomorrow. The tents are lightweight and you can bang the pegs into the ice. What's up?' Massey suddenly realized that David was staring at him.

'Nothing. It's – it's just that your hands are shaking.'

Massey steadied them but they soon began again. 'It's an old accident,' he said quickly.

'Accident?'

'Got them frost-bitten. I was lucky – my fingers were saved, but it left me with the shakes. Doesn't happen all the time.'

David remembered how Massey had saved the crew of the helicopter. The rescue had clearly left him with emotional scars, but the way Massey handled these only added to David's respect for the man.

5

Even Gerry had not realized the going would be so rough. He could see the penguin rookery – and still smell and hear it – and the snow-clad mountains rising behind, but their summits looked so far away, crowded with black, gaunt rock and scree, and with glaciers coursing down their sides. He knew they were frozen rivers, moving fractionally, but they were dark this morning and sinister in the overcast conditions. Terns flew low and fast over the penguins and, away from the glaciers and the snow melt, lichens clung to the rocks of the mountainsides.

In the bay, the dark water was sultry white with icebergs. A new shelf of ice had broken off the mainland and was drifting slowly out to sea. Without the refracting light, the desolation at the end of the world was intense. Nevertheless, Gerry felt elated and physically fit, despite the rigours of the previous night, and he was invigorated by the rawness of the mountains and the stunted micro-life that struggled for existence on their rocky slopes.

David, however, was tired and depressed,

darting glances at Steve to see how he was faring, his feeling of apprehension growing. The wind had only slightly gathered in strength, blowing on shore, the chill factor not great but announcing its presence by every so often penetrating his protective clothing. The clouds were ominously darkening, a shade at a time, and the skuas flew overhead threateningly, as if these enormous gulls had confused them all with the luckless chinstrap chicks below. Fire and ice – the words kept battering his mind. This was the beginning and the end. The ancient volcanos. The intensity of the fire. The deadly chill of the ice. This was where life had begun; where it had ended. The days were long, plunging into twilight but never into proper darkness, yet he knew that in the Antarctic winter, beginning in July, the pack ice would form, the bay freeze over, the darkness come and the place would die. When hell freezes over, he thought. But it was bad enough in the summer, with this praying mantis of a wind.

He also had the unnerving impression that the mountain they were so slowly and painfully climbing was a living entity, with its own pulse beat and a constantly changing outer skin, rather like a monstrous animal that was growing or shedding new patches of protection every day, every minute. The mountain still held the snows of last winter, frozen sand and scree which formed into treacherous mud-slides. According to Massey, the melt could occasionally even send black boulders tumbling down to the beach, but because there was little sun at the moment the ground was slightly firmer than it usually was. Nevertheless, David found the going hard; his snowboots continually slipped and he often seemed to be making more progress going down than up, the crumbling surface producing a depressing – and often dangerous – game of snakes and ladders. He began to be terrified by the possibility of one of the black rocks becoming dislodged and grinding him into the crust of the mountainside.

After a while Massey came to a halt. 'We've got to make a decision now,' he said. No-one spoke – even Steve – for in such an awesome landscape there was no doubt that Tom Massey was captain, king and god. What would happen to us if anything happened to him? thought David. How terrible it would be if we were out here alone. He glanced at Steve who was quiet and reflective. He showed no sign of physical strain while David himself was breathing all too heavily, the sweat building up in his snowshoes and under his polar suit. It was difficult to get used to this warm wetness, rather as if he had pissed himself, although pissing oneself was the allowable thing to do. Steve had either built himself up to a tremendous degree of physical fitness during his arduous adventures in Wales, or he had natural stamina – perhaps a combination of both. Either way, David felt terrified that he was not going to be able to keep up with the others. He looked at Gerry, hoping for a fellow sufferer, but with his long legs and weekly training for long-distance running he probably had more of a chance. He seemed to be breathing quite naturally and was looking alert and comfortable as he stared up at the black volcanic gloom of the mountain peak.

'We need to cross that eroded glacier up there,' said Massey. 'We'll have to cut steps in it with our ice axes – I'll show you how – and then go sideways like crabs. Anyone suffer from vertigo?' His gaze swept their faces. David shook his head.

Gerry didn't like heights but he had never suffered from vertigo before. A wave of insecurity shook him. Would this be the first time?

Traversing the glacier was not nearly as bad as David had imagined, for the ice was firm and covered with dried mud which gave his snowshoes a strong grip. His axe bit into the ice deeply, and although he didn't dare to look down, he felt safe. In fact, traversing was much better than the slippery climb up, which was so exhausting and emotionally draining as false crest merged into false crest.

'You OK?' he asked Gerry.

'Yeah,' was the muttered reply.

David knew that it wasn't the climbing that was affecting Gerry, but the height.

'You sure?'

'Trying not to look down. Don't talk.'

'Sorry.'

Gerry staggered and began to fall.

But he didn't go far. Hanging on to his ice axe which acted as a brace, he slipped into a small gully. Then David saw to his horror that below the mud-caked, moist earth was a sheer drop.

'Don't move,' said Massey. He turned to Steve. 'Go on. You know what to do.'

Steve cautiously inched his way down, grabbed Gerry's legs and almost effortlessly swung him back on to the glacier. The whole operation took a few seconds.

'Thanks,' Gerry gasped. 'Can I take a rest?'

'No,' replied Massey firmly. 'Keep going. We'll have a break once we're on the snow.'

As they edged their way over, David could see that Gerry's body was taut with nervous tension. Nevertheless, they all made it safely to the snow and were soon looking up towards the summit, bathed in sweat, their skis slung across their shoulders and their axes flashing polished steel in the sun that had just broken through the clouds. The sun made all the difference, turning the glacier opalescent with cobalt blue as its main colour, and the snow on the mountain sparkling green and white. Even the black peaks seemed to shine and the flooding light was a psychological boost to them all. It was like coming out of a shadowed world into sparkling brilliance that promised welcome and safety and achievement.

'Well done, everybody.' Massey was warmly approving but Gerry felt ashamed.

'Sorry about that.'

'Why sorry? You handled it well. In this kind of environment the important thing is how you handle your mistakes.'

'That's right.' Steve spoke for the first time in hours and both Gerry and David noticed the difference in him immediately. Since the rescue, he had become much more a figure of authority, a second in command. Quite a contrast to the paranoia of last night, thought David, remembering how he had torn the note into little pieces and shoved it into the fire when the others had gone outside.

They ate biscuits, bully beef and drank bottled water at lunchtime, still on the snow before making their ascent to the peak.

The going was becoming ever more treacherous now for the face of the mountain was covered in scree and it was impossible to tell the more solid earth from mud and debris and dirty ice. The climbing was tortuous but exhilarating, and David, with his new-found physical confidence, used his ice axe as a metal claw to pull himself up higher and higher on the slippery, unpredictable surface. Quite often he slid as the slope gave way under his feet, but he began to pride himself on getting his axe impacted as tightly as possible, seeking hard ground rather than the crumbling moraine. Below him, the drop was less severe than on the face of the glacier, falling away more gently.

After a while, Gerry found himself climbing alongside Steve. Gerry, too, had been wondering about Steve's state of mind, but had been considerably reassured by his new calm assertiveness.

'How's it going?' asked Steve kindly.

'All right.'

'I'm sweating like a pig.' He grinned at Gerry. 'But it's good out here. I feel OK outside. It's inside I get bad. Start to think things.'

'Tom Massey's a good leader, isn't he?' Gerry wanted to test the water, to see whether Steve was really becoming more stable or whether it was all on the surface. 'I remember my dad used to talk about him a lot. He'd been on other expeditions with him and he thought Massey was fantastic. I think David's father felt the same.'

'He's OK.'

'What was he like in Wales?'

'Like this at first,' Steve replied ominously.

'And then?'

'A sod.'

'What changed him?'

'Nothing.'

'Don't get you.'

'I told you, mate, he's two people.' He looked up at Massey's athletic form, some distance above them.

'Schizoid?' Gerry felt depressed. Steve hadn't changed at all.

'It's not funny.' There was cold conviction in his voice. 'Once he goes, he goes.'

'What do you mean?'

'He can be like this for a long time. Then it's as if he's been shut off; someone else comes into his mind and slams the door.'

'You shouldn't talk like that,' said Gerry reprovingly. 'Massey's been so good to you – and to us over our dads.'

'That someone is a monster,' continued Steve as if Gerry hadn't spoken. 'I'm warning you, that's all.'

On the summit there were great spires – almost like stalagmites – thrusting towards the sky and illuminated by the sun into blues and greens and pinks. Despite his exhaustion, David thought they were utterly beautiful.

On the other side was a frozen plateau, lustrous and gleaming. Massey radioed the *Patriot*, telling the wireless operator all was well, while the three boys watched the swirling clouds coming in from the glitteringly cold sea, fleetingly obscuring the sun and turning the mountains dun-coloured and sombre.

'It's four,' said Massey, 'and you've done superbly. We'll hack it over the next glacier now. But watch it – once we get on to the snow again there'll be crevasses and they're not easy to spot.' His voice tailed away and then picked up quickly. 'Don't be complacent,' he warned.

'We're certainly not that,' said Steve aggressively.

David's heart sank, for the hostility was back in Steve's voice. Was he tired, or had the exhilaration of the climbing temporarily overshadowed his obsession? He would have liked to believe it was the former.

'One more point,' said Massey, seemingly oblivious of Steve's hostility. 'The wind's getting up.'

Clearly the weather in the Antarctic was all too unpredictable, for after being dormant for so long the wind quadrupled its speed in a few seconds, changing its lurking mood for a full frontal attack. Immediately the bitterness of its cold breath pierced their polar suits.

'Let's get down to the plateau. We'll find shelter there.' Massey sounded hopeful, but after trekking for another couple of hours over the glacier they arrived on a rocky escarpment that looked down to a snow- and ice-filled valley that rose again to a scree-covered mountainside. This was much more sheer than the one they had just crossed. 'Rothera Base is over the summit and down the other slope, but if this turns into a blizzard we'll make camp soon. We've got enough supplies for five or six days so we can be confident. But don't worry – these blizzards are quick jobs in the summer and it should be over by the morning, and that's being pessimistic.'

David felt better after this speech and took the sudden snow storm in his stride, although the heightened keening of the wind made putting up the insulated survival tent extremely difficult. It was hard to bang the pegs into the ground which was frozen solid, but eventually they managed it. They huddled inside as the twilight drew in, the wind increased and the snow piled up around the tent in huge drifts, but once the calor gas stove was going and the four of them had food inside them, the situation seemed much less threatening.

'We'll get some sleep after we've had cocoa,' said Massey. 'If this does lift in the morning, we'll need to make an early start.'

Despite a further increase in the wind strength and the howling it made amongst the crags and rocks, Gerry and David slept dreamlessly until dawn when they both woke refreshed – to find that not only were Tom Massey's and Steve's sleeping bags empty, but they were cold as well. Peering blearily out of the tent in rising alarm, they could see only a totally white landscape with the rocks covered in driven snow, the wind still blowing strongly and no trace of the missing members of the expedition.

A wave of panic hit David and seemed to swallow him up; he couldn't speak, couldn't do anything but stare out at the unsullied snow.

'What's happened?' Gerry crouched beside him and David could sense the fear rising in him too.

'How the hell do I know?'

'There's no footsteps, but I guess the snow would cover them up immediately.'

'That's right.' A rush of relief flooded through David. Why was he panicking? Of course, there *had* to be a logical explanation and that was it. 'But why have they gone off like that?'

'To have a pee?'

'He said to do that round the back of the tent.'

There was no immediate answer and both Gerry and David remained staring out at the unmarked snow.

'Wait a minute,' said David.

'What's up?'

'Something's sticking out – over there.'

73

Pulling on their protective clothing, they hurried outside; immediately the wind-chill hit them, its physical force probing and relentless.

Half-buried in the shifting snow of a little gully was a snowshoe. It was Steve's.

'What the hell is this doing here?' Gerry was aghast. 'He can't have dropped it,' he finished ludicrously.

'Dropped a shoe?' David laughed with a degree of hysteria and then fought for control. 'Don't be ridiculous.'

'Where is he?'

'No marks.'

'That's because of the wind—'

'All right. All right.' They were both panicking now.

'Didn't Massey say there was a cave?'

'An ice cave?' David clawed at the idea. 'I can't remember him saying anything of the kind.'

'What about the overhang?'

They ploughed through the loose snow, hardly able to see as the wind whipped it up in their faces.

'Nothing here.'

'Wait.' Gerry looked down and moved forward.

'Don't go near the edge,' David barked in a shrill voice that he would ever afterwards be ashamed of.

'OK. There it is – I think.'

Icicles were like a thick spider's web hanging from a snow-covered boulder.

'Could there be a cave under there?'

'Let's go and see.' David wanted action of any kind – action that would lead to some kind of resolution.

'Careful—'

But Gerry was too late as David stepped forward and plunged out of sight. There was the sound of slithering and then a dull thump.

'You OK?'

'Yeah.'

'Sure?'

'I'm fine. I'm on a ledge. Can you work your way down?'

Gerry grabbed the ice, wincing as the cold penetrated his gloves, and slid down, landing with a crunch just in front of David who was standing staring at the blackness inside the cave.

'We should have brought a torch,' he began.

'No need.'

'Why?' What was wrong with David's voice? Gerry wondered. He sounded so abrupt, unnerved.

'I can see the other snowboot.' David moved cautiously forward. 'And I think there's a foot inside it.'

Steve was dead. He was also almost frozen solid, with a knife driven up to its hilt in his chest.

He looked completely unreal, like a waxwork in the Chamber of Horrors, yet David knew there was no escape from the fact that this was Steve – and Steve had been murdered.

'God,' said Gerry. 'Please, God. No.' He vomited into the snow and then began to give out a series of dry sobs. When he had finished there was a seemingly eternal, unbelieving silence.

David gently brushed the masking snow off Steve's face to reveal his lips drawn back in a snarl.

'He didn't give up that easily,' whispered David. 'At least, I don't think he did.'

'Who could have done it?'

'Wait a minute – what's this?' David bent down and picked up a pair of goggles.

Gerry stared at him numbly. 'I've never seen them before. They don't belong to Massey – or to Steve. And they're a foreign make. Isn't this Spanish?'

'Who the hell attacked him?' asked David. 'Is someone following us?'

'Why should they?' answered Gerry.

David was shaking now as the shock reached him and his thoughts raced so fast that they were just a noisy clamour in his head.

'Where is Massey? Suppose he's dead too.' David stuttered out the words. 'Suppose he's—' But then they heard a familiar voice above them.

'What are you two doing?' The tone was irritable, anxious and therefore reassuring. Massey hurried on, without waiting for an answer. 'I'm searching for Steve. I've been up for hours and still can't find him. You seen him? And what are you both *doing* down there?'

There didn't seem to be any adequate reply.

'You'd better see for yourself,' said David eventually.

6

'What's up?' Then Massey saw Steve. 'Jesus.'

He went down on his knees and began to weep.
David and Gerry stood there, helplessly watching
him. The weeping became long, harsh, wracking
sobs, rather like Gerry's. He ran his gloved fore-
finger gently over Steve's face. 'I've been searching
for him,' he repeated. 'I never thought he'd go this
far.'

Who? wondered David. What was Massey talking about?

'How long?' asked Gerry.

'Couple of hours. I woke up and saw Steve was
gone. God knows what he thought he was doing,
getting up and going out in these conditions.'

'Why didn't you wake us?'

'I didn't think he'd gone far. Just for a pee or a
think or whatever.'

'He's been murdered,' said David in desperation. 'Can't you see? Someone's killed him.
And we found these goggles – there's a Spanish
trademark on them.'

'It's that bastard Martinez. Chris Martinez.'

Gerry and David looked at Massey blankly. What could he be talking about? Who was this man they had never heard of? They were both in shock and their minds seemed as frozen as the landscape. Steve? Dead? It was unbelievable.

'Who's—'

But Massey wasn't listening, still staring down at the dead, frozen face, seemingly unaware of the question – punching the goggles in his hand until he broke the plastic.

'Who *is* he?' yelled Gerry. 'This Martinez—'

'He's an Anglo-Argentine from a company called Polar Exploration.'

'So?'

'Martinez was looking for the same mineral belt your dads were searching for. The bastard.' Massey stared up at them, his eyes still full of tears. He looked completely broken. 'He tried to buy me but I wasn't telling him a damn thing. He reckons I'm after the bloody minerals myself – said he'd kill me if I came here again. He got Steve instead.' He bowed his head, stroking away the shimmering particles of ice on the frozen forehead.

'But did our fathers find anything?'

'I'm not sure, but Martinez thinks they did. Steve's murder is a warning to me – to provide information I haven't got.'

'Why didn't you tell us about this guy?' asked Gerry. 'Did my dad know him?'

'Of him. None of us took him seriously – least of all me. I wouldn't have brought you here if I had. He must be crazy. God.' Massey put his hands over his eyes, rocking himself to and fro. 'Please, God, no. First your fathers. Now him.'

'Did Martinez kill them too?'

'No – he was nowhere near when it happened. Do you think I'd just let him get away with it if he had?' said Massey angrily.

Gerry didn't reply and David was thinking, If only I'd shown him the note. If only we could have taken a shared decision.

'Let's go and see if there's any trace of anyone,' said David, knowing he had to talk to Gerry alone.

'No,' said Massey sharply. 'This man's dangerous. Can't you understand that?'

'Is he representing his company?'

'No. His own interests. What else?' He leant over Steve again and David didn't think he had ever seen anyone in such mental agony before.

'Will you radio up a helicopter?' asked Gerry.

'In this?' Massey looked incredulous and Gerry immediately felt a fool. 'We'll have to get to Rothera. I've got no weapons, nothing.' He seemed to have slightly lost his grip. 'He'll be out there. Coming for us.'

'Us?'

'If the weather eases up a bit we'll go for the base as fast as we can.'

81

David intervened. 'There's something I've got to tell you. Both of you.'

'Yes?'

Gerry looked at him curiously as if he thought he could never have any secrets.

'I should have told you this before.'

'What are you talking about?' barked Massey. 'Don't try to hold out on me.'

'Steve left me a note that first night in the hut.'

'Well?'

'He said – he thought you were going to kill him.'

Gerry gazed at David as if he had made it all up. But Massey nodded, as if he immediately understood, and grew much calmer.

There was a long, long silence. Then he said quietly, 'Poor sod.'

'What?' David couldn't understand what he meant.

'Poor sod.' Massey was reflective now. 'Steve was paranoid. Too badly damaged – way before I could work on him. And now that bastard Martinez has got him.' He paused and they saw a sudden tragic realization in his eyes. 'Of course,' he muttered.

David shivered. As the numbness faded the fear was beginning to grip him, as sharp as the wind above them. Were they all going to be picked off by this prowling marauder?

'My main concern is that this guy is close and I have to protect you. These mineral rights could make him a fortune—'

'He won't kill you, if he thinks you can lead him to wherever they are,' said David sceptically.

'He will eventually. I told you, he's killed Steve as a warning – to me personally.'

'And we could be next,' said Gerry. Neither of them could really believe they were actually having this conversation. But they were. What had started as a nerve-wracking but well-planned expedition in an alien environment had turned out to be a disaster.

'I'll protect you,' said Massey, regaining a shadow of his normal confidence. 'With my bare hands if necessary. And that knife, in case you were going to ask, is Steve's.'

'Yes,' said Gerry. 'I recognized it.'

'I'll radio the *Patriot* and tell them what's happened.'

They were all shivering now, even in the shelter of the cave. Gerry and David were still deeply shocked. Neither of them had seen death before and had hardly dared imagine it. To David, Steve simply wasn't there any longer, his features expressionless, but the brutality of the killing was appalling. He would never hear Steve's Liverpudlian tones again, and although he had been wary – frightened of him even – the shock of him passing out of existence so abruptly was incredible.

Slowly, the realization of the danger to their own lives began to return.

'What I still don't understand,' said Gerry, 'is why this Martinez character would kill him just because he wants to know where these minerals are. Anyway, you've already told him you don't know.'

'He didn't believe me.'

'And he'll stalk us?' demanded David. 'Pick us off one by one as a way of proving he means business?'

'I'm not saying he'll go any further,' said Massey. 'And if we stick together at all times, I can protect you.'

'Against a gun?'

'Who said he's got one? He killed Steve with his own knife.'

'That was quieter,' said David.

'He could have a gun with a silencer,' pointed out Gerry. 'Anyway, what the hell are we talking about? There's no-one to hear anything, help anyone, out here.'

They gazed at each other hopelessly.

'And there's something else.' David was struggling to think a little more clearly. 'Why didn't you just tell this Martinez where our fathers had been researching and just leave it up to him?'

'Because if it *is* there it's an important discovery that should belong to the UK, in their memory, not end up an Argentine coup.'

'Why hasn't there been another expedition set up to find these minerals?' asked David impatiently.

'There've been two others, but they both drew a blank.'

'Weren't you consulted?'

'Of course.'

'Didn't – weren't you able to tell them exactly *where* our fathers were searching?' asked Gerry.

'Yes.' Massey gazed at them confidently.

'Well?'

'I told you. They drew a blank.'

'But Martinez thinks you *do* know. How's that?'

'I thought he was a friend. I told him a bit about our expedition and I was a fool. But I do have a clue about the mineral belt, although I could be wrong.'

'Where is it then?' asked David.

'One place your dads were particularly interested in was a small ice cave, not much bigger then this, at the bottom of a crevasse.'

'The one they fell into?'

'No.' He paused. 'They seemed excited, but they'd been like that before and we'd gone a long way, looked at a good many possibilities. But I always had a feeling they didn't go far enough. The crevasse is deep and needs expert climbers to get down there not geologists, however fit they are, whatever risks they're prepared to take. It's only a possibility – one that I could check out myself using some equipment from the base if we have time. If not, I'll get the job done. You can be sure of that.'

'And Martinez is prepared to kill for a possibility?' asked David.

'He doesn't know where this crevasse is – I deliberately refused to give him the exact location so that it could be a British discovery – have your fathers' names.'

'That would be fantastic,' said Gerry.

'Please try and have faith in me. I know it's difficult.' Massey sounded bitter.

'We've got absolute faith in you,' reassured Gerry and David backed him up. 'Listen – you mustn't take on so much responsibility, Tom. You have to share it, however raw we are.' For the first time he felt he was reaching Massey on a more equal level.

'I know it's difficult to believe that this Martinez character would go to such lengths,' Massey continued.

For the first time since they had begun the discussion, David glanced down at Steve's body – and then quickly looked away again.

'Mineral rights are illegal under the Antarctic Treaty but that wouldn't stop him. And he's a geologist. He'd make his name. Have the crevasse called after him. Think of the personal prestige.'

'Can he climb?'

'Yes.'

'But you're still not sure, are you?' asked Gerry. 'You're still not sure if there are minerals in that cave.'

'No.' Massey shook his head. 'I'm not sure.'

'So Martinez is taking a risk.'

'It's all a risk,' said Massey dismissively.

'But he needs to know the exact location,' David persisted.

'He'd do anything to get it. As you can see, he's given me a terrible warning for holding out. He was battering at me in the UK – came to see me, pleading, offering money – and when I wouldn't agree, he started issuing threats. I didn't take him seriously or I would never have brought you here. Never.'

'And he's close. Won't we see him? It must be impossible to keep out of sight in a place like this,' demanded David.

'Easy for an expert. Martinez has climbed out here for years. He knows the landscape intimately.'

'Shouldn't we go back? asked Gerry in un-characteristic panic. 'Couldn't we get the Zenith and go like hell for the *Patriot*?'

'No, our only bet is Rothera. We'd be just as much at risk going back.' He was adamant.

'There's something else Steve told us,' said Gerry. 'I tried to tell you but you wouldn't let me.'

'Well?' He sounded more exhausted than apprehensive.

'He said he'd listened in to a call, and that he hadn't liked what he heard. The call sounds as if it must have come from Martinez.'

'It did. He phoned several times, offering me money and making veiled threats about what could happen if I didn't fully co-operate. I suppose Steve listened in on the extension in my sitting-room. Typical. He *had* to be one up. I was the boss so he had to find something to hold over me.'

Poor old Steve, thought David. Wrecked by his paranoia. David felt a great weakness inside him. They had miles of icy terrain to cover before they could rejoin the *Patriot*. Was he going to be able to hack it?

'What are we going to do with the body?' asked Gerry.

'There'll be an official inquiry – we must leave him exactly as he is.'

'Police – out here?' David was incredulous.

'The Royal Navy.' Massey's voice broke and he again knelt down by Steve, taking his frozen hand and stroking his hair. 'I'm sorry,' he whispered. 'I'm so sorry I couldn't protect you better than this.' Then Massey got up and looked at Gerry and David steadily. 'We've been out here far too long. We'll get back to the tent and make some decisions.' He picked up the goggles and put them in his pocket. 'Don't worry – we'll get that bastard.'

By the time they had brewed up coffee and had had something to eat, some of the shock had at least eased, but it left a dull and gnawing ache which wouldn't go away. Steve had been a threat; now he was dead, he seemed even more of one.

Massey, meanwhile, gave them an impassioned speech that was full of concern and authority and logic.

'I've got to try and reassure you but I know it's difficult not to lose confidence in a situation like this. I knew your dads very well last year, and if I haven't talked much about them, then it's because I still find it too painful. And now there's Steve—' He paused and then forced himself to carry on. 'You both take after your fathers in interesting ways. Adam was an adventurer, a loner – someone who could never follow the crowd. He had a special kind of integrity and I knew I could always trust him. He'd never bullshit or put anyone down. Peter was much more of a joiner – easier company sometimes, I suppose. He'd got a good dry sense of humour and he was ambitious – far more ambitious than Adam. He wanted to make that mineral discovery, while Adam was just there for the purity of geological exploration. To encapsulate the difference between them, Peter would always have a party to celebrate anything – and Adam's kind of celebration was a long walk on his own.'

I wish Dad could have been more outgoing with me, thought David, while Gerry felt proud that much of what he had always respected about his father had rubbed off on Massey.

Eventually the decision was made to continue as the wind had died back a little and the snow flurries were slight. Nevertheless, visibility was bad. There was no shadow on the dead white surface of the plateau, which to both Gerry and David's eyes looked uniformly level.

'We'll be able to ski for a while,' Massey said. 'But keep in my tracks.'

They gradually descended the undulating slope from the plateau to the valley. The skiing was easy, but they both found themselves getting drowsy as the morning wore on into early afternoon. Steve's murder was still at the front of their minds and his dead face seemed to overshadow the treacherous landscape. Small depressions escaped their attention and more than once either Gerry or David almost fell as they hit a snow mound.

Despite their goggles, the strain on their eyes was enormous and David became more and more exhausted. Gradually he fell behind and then, half dozing, lost control and swung across the tracks and out into the virgin snow. Within seconds he had realized what had happened and was about to turn back towards his companions in another wide arc when Massey yelled out, '*Stop!*'

Flustered, David continued to turn.

'What?'

'There's a crevasse.'

He tried to snow-plough, his ski tips touching and his heels hard out, but he was too late. David plunged towards the crack in the ice and began to fall.

His skis saved him from going straight into the abyss, straddling the ice before sinking slowly through, giving him time to grip the snow-covered rock as he gazed down. It was dark at the bottom but the sides were curved, giving his skis some purchase. Then, like a chute in a fairground, he found himself slowly slipping. He screamed, feeling his skis cutting through ice, his body weight bearing him down and sliding towards the chasm.

No-one came and he was still slipping, seeing Steve's dead face. Now one ski was sliding more than the other. Ice broke, snow slipped, and with a scream of terror David plunged down another couple of metres, his hands covered in powder and unable to grip – driven forward. He yelled out again and again – and continued to slide.

The relentless slow descent continued. Was that a crystal he could see at the bottom of the black abyss? There was something there. Not a crystal. A face. Dad's face and a beckoning hand with the signet ring that he had half-forgotten his father always wore. He could even hear his voice again: 'David.'

'I'm coming.'

'Hurry up, old son.'

'I'm coming, Dad.'

'David.' But the voice wasn't his father's. Who was calling? It was so confusing.

'I've got you. I'm going to pull you backwards.'

'Yes.'

'Come on, old son.'

His father's face disappeared, the crystal glowed and then there was only darkness.

'I was slipping.'

'You had one leg wedged tightly. You wouldn't have gone that far.'

David was lying on the snow, his skis off, Gerry and Massey kneeling beside him. Just as they had knelt around Steve, he thought, but with a different look in their eyes. A kind of wonder.

'I kept looking back,' Massey kept repeating. 'But clearly not enough.'

'It wasn't your fault,' said Gerry. 'So did I – but he was off course in a few seconds.'

'Sorry,' said David inadequately.

'It's OK.' Massey looked down at him reassuringly and David saw the light of concern in his eyes. 'Look, both of you. We're going to make camp just before the valley. We started too late and you're both exhausted.'

'I can go on,' insisted David.

'What about Martinez?' Gerry was anxious. 'We'll be such an easy target.'

'I know a place that's hard to find – a small ravine we can use – and we can take turns as lookout. It's the only thing we can do. It's far too dangerous to go on – and look at the visibility. This isn't just twilight; it has all the makings of that blizzard we've been waiting for.'

They skied on in the dwindling light until the going became too rough. Frozen rocks pierced the deep snow and they had to take off their skis and trudge on in snowboots.

'Not much further,' said Massey encouragingly. 'Tomorrow morning, all we have to do is to cross the valley and climb the mountain and the base is on the other side. We can check out the cave, build the cairn, and then radio up a helicopter. That way we can be back on the *Patriot* either tomorrow night or early the next morning.' He made it all sound extraordinarily easy.

'There's no-one at the base, is there?' asked David.

93

'No.'

Not even Martinez? thought Gerry.

They struggled down for another hour until the slope flattened out into a small plateau. The wind was screaming now, howling around them at a far greater rate than it had been before. They were freezing cold and their lips, despite protective cream, were raw and torn.

'We'll pitch here,' said Massey. He was right. There was a very small depression. Ravine was too grand a term.

Somehow they got the tent up just as the driving snow began to increase and their surroundings slowly lost all definition.

David had never felt so cold in his life, and his fingers and toes were numb. As they thawed out alarmingly slowly around the calor-gas stove, Gerry winced.

'I'm afraid it'll be painful as the circulation comes back,' Massey sympathized.

David felt the shooting pains and tried to prevent himself crying out.

'Get some of this on your lips.' Massey passed round a freezing-cold jar of glutinous liquid. 'Kind of high-powered Vaseline; it'll work itself into the cracks. Surprising how quickly they heal up.'

We're totally reliant on him, thought David. Suppose he disappears or Martinez catches up with him – we'd be alone in this freezing wilderness without the slightest idea of how to get to the base.

'Do you reckon Martinez is close?' asked Gerry, putting David's thoughts unpleasantly into words.

'He could be. He's probably camped out like we are. I'm not minimizing the situation – I'm being completely honest with you. But as long as this wind continues to blast the snow about, then he won't get to us. Not a chance. This is a real white-out, and I have to warn you that it could last.'

'How long?' asked David.

'I don't know, but we'll be safe here – snug as bugs in rugs. We've got plenty of food and protection.'

'And then?' demanded Gerry.

'Then we're going to take a slightly longer, slightly more difficult back-route over that mountain. Just in case he's around. I'll tell the *Patriot* what's going on, and directly this weather's over they'll send out the chopper to do a reconnaissance.' He went to the tent flap and they heard him giving the call sign. 'Come in, Alpha Lima. Come in, Alpha Lima.'

'This is Alpha Lima, Bravo Snowbound. How are you doing? Over.'

'We have a— Hello, Alpha Lima? I've lost you. Come in, Alpha Lima. Come in. Come in.'

But there was only a mass of static.

'What's the problem?' asked Gerry.

'Weather.' Massey tried again and again but couldn't raise the *Patriot* at all. 'I'll try again in the morning,' he told them.

The persistent angry howling of the wind reminded David of a large and hungry animal that was baying outside, all too anxious to tear its way into the tent and rip their throats out.

They prepared a meal of soup, corned-beef hash and cocoa. The food was comforting, a physical barrier to the shrieking animal outside which was fast becoming Martinez as well – a terrifying combination which might walk in on them at any time, particularly during the night.

They got into their bags, tense and apprehensive. Gerry couldn't get Steve's dead face out of his mind. Then, just as he was drifting into sleep, he began to wonder if Massey was too confident. Suppose – just suppose – Martinez was out there now, slowly coming towards them on the soft, concealing snow. They wouldn't hear him – until it was too late.

Gerry tried to shake off the unsettling idea. He wasn't the imaginative type like David and he usually had himself far more together than this. He glanced across at Massey, lying in his bag, the lamp reflecting his long dark hair and his chiselled, almost stereotypical hero's features. He looked enormously reassuring.

Suddenly Massey spoke out of the darkness. 'I'd like to say a prayer for him. I'm not much good at organized religion but I've got my own belief. Does anyone mind?'

They murmured their acquiesence and he said slowly and quietly, 'We pray for Steve's soul. Please, God – let him rest in peace.'

7

Eventually David stopped shivering and the damp warmth of his clothing combined with the womb-like nest of the sleeping bag took him over, and even the wind, still shrieking amongst the rocks, seemed slightly less threatening. But what had really helped were Massey's final words that night: 'Just before you go to sleep – and you *need* to sleep – remember this: whether or not we stay here for another day is irrelevant; you'll be as comfortable and as warm as you are now. And I can assure you, Martinez won't get anywhere near us in this weather. You're safe. I'm sorry, desperately sorry, about what's happened and your involvement in it, particularly after the tragedy of your fathers' deaths. I'm grieving for Steve and directly you're safely back on the *Patriot* I'll be out with the helicopter crew. We'll pick him up and bring him back to the UK for a decent burial. We'll also get that bastard Martinez. So – despite everything – please have faith in me.'

David snuggled deeper into his bag. He had the strange feeling that the wind was now an old beggar woman, howling a lullaby to her waif children.

'David?'

'Mm.'

'Dave!'

'What is it?'

'Massey's gone.'

David sat up, his heart thumping. The nightmare was becoming circular.

'Is his bag cold? Like Steve's was?' he asked, feeling muddled and disorientated. Steve was dead. Massey was dead, his scrambled brain told him.

'No. It's warm.'

'He must be having a pee then.' Hope surged and David felt a glow of comfort and normality. Life couldn't, mustn't be as punitive as this.

'I woke up and couldn't see the hump any longer.'

'This is like a detective story. They keep disappearing and turning up dead.' David tried the feeble joke but wished he hadn't.

Gerry didn't laugh. 'The wind's lessening.'

'We must get out there.' David dragged himself out of his bag. 'He's dead,' he added, his control slipping away completely.

'Shut up!' snapped Gerry. 'If you can't say anything constructive, just keep your feeble mouth shut.'

'We'll get back, though. We'll get back without him.'

'Of course we bloody well can't.' Gerry was always the realist.

'I know what to do. I can get you back—' David was almost sobbing in his panic as they struggled into their polar suits, bumping into each other like two lunar spacemen who had lost their gravity.

Outside there was a full moon in a crystal heaven, the stars glittering icily. The snow stretched around them, occasionally blowing into flurries but basically like a dead white desert stretching into infinity. Below them was a wide valley, a glacier covering it like a shroud, its tail running down from the gaunt black rock of the mountain they had to climb. An icy fog hung over the glacier like a giant's breath, giving it a false height and deadly smoothness. The whole place was so hostile that David felt he could hardly breathe. Worse still, there was absolutely no sign of Massey.

'Footprints?' muttered Gerry.

'Too much flying snow. It's Steve all over again.'

'No way.'

'*Why* don't you stop fooling yourself?' David had still not regained his nerve.

'And why are you always such a bloody pessimist?'

David was silent. Both of them were beginning

to realize that the argument was a release for their emotions and a little island of distraction against the elements around them, and did nothing to check the sudden antipathy they felt for each other.

'Bastard,' returned David.

'You wimp.'

David rushed at Gerry, arms flailing, only to find that his new enemy was pointing over his shoulder.

'Here he comes!' he yelled.

'What?'

'Massey. Tom Massey, you moon-faced idiot.'

Above them, the real moon starkly illuminated the stumbling figure.

'Tom?'

Still he hurried towards them. Was he limping? Was he staggering? Was it Massey?

'Careful, in case it's not him,' cautioned David.

'It *is* him.'

'You sure?'

They stood stock still, aware that it could be anyone, and because of the distance problem they both found enormous difficulty in assessing how near the figure actually was. Then he waved.

'It *must* be him,' affirmed David.

'Let's be certain. Stay here with me.' Now it was Gerry's turn to be careful. 'We should have a weapon.'

'I've got one—' David held up his ice axe.

The figure continued to hurry rather erratically towards them.

'How much longer is this going to take?' worried Gerry.

'Wait. I think I can see—' David wanted to be absolutely sure. There must be no mistake. Then he knew there wasn't. 'It's Massey. I can see his beard,' he said with relief.

'Beards are common.'

David laughed. 'I didn't realize you were such a snob.'

'I *mean*, he's not the only man with a beard.'

'No. This is Massey all right.'

And it was.

Within seconds he was gasping and panting in front of them and they could see that he had a bad cut on his forehead, showing livid in the bleached moonlight.

'Sorry.' He could hardly speak.

'What's happened?'

'I thought someone was out there.'

'Were they?' asked David fearfully.

'Yes.'

'Martinez?'

'I'm afraid so. The wind had dropped, so he decided on a little night excursion.'

'Where's he camped?' asked Gerry anxiously.

'He was below the ridge. I sent him packing.'

'Did he have a gun?'

'Can't have. I'd be done for if he had.' He bent down, panting, trying to regain his breath.

'Why didn't you tell us you were going out?' Gerry was partly concerned, partly angry.

'I thought it might be a false alarm.'

Back in the tent, Massey rubbed his hands warm while the little calor-gas stove spluttered. The cut on his head was bad, not bleeding now but crusted over.

'What did he hit you with?'

'Tent pole.'

'You went to his camp?'

'I followed him back. At first he didn't see me. Then he did.'

'You mean he was spying on us?' asked Gerry.

'Yes. Checking us out.'

'For an attack?'

'Maybe. Anyway, directly he saw me he *did* attack. I was a fool, I didn't take a weapon with me. We had a bit of a punch-up – which went to me in the end.'

'Are you OK?'

'Sure. Only a crack on the head. Can't go septic out here. Just freezes over.'

'Where's Martinez now?'

'He made off, so I immobilized his tent.'

'How?' asked Gerry.

'Chucked it down a crevasse.' Massey chuckled. 'Rather unsporting but par for the course. He was skiing down into the valley, going like the clappers. Without protection he'll have to make for the Argentine base at Datio Sound.'

'So you reckon we've seen the last of him?' David was bewildered by the speed of events and ashamed of the incident with Gerry. He had to have more resources.

'I hope so. We'll get up early and go like hell. If we don't make the base, or the weather closes in again, we'll pitch the tent for another night.'

Massey struggled into his bag and with relief the others followed.

'Shouldn't you put a dressing on that cut?' asked Gerry sleepily.

'I will in the morning – when I've thawed out a bit.' Massey turned over then snuggled down. The wind had died away almost completely now and there was a new and rather uneasy feeling of temporary calm to the silent world outside.

Tom Massey muttered and threshed about in his bag until he finally woke Gerry – and eventually David. They lay there, listening to him, not able to make out what he was saying. Then he began to call out the two familiar, painful names.

'Adam. Peter.'

They made no attempt to wake him, but the pain inside them was hard to bear.

'Adam.'

Gerry tried to get out of his sleeping bag but David signalled him back.

Massey's voice died away into incoherent muttering. 'I can see you down there, but I can't get to you!' he shouted suddenly. 'Can you hear me? He's gone. I'm sorry. Terribly sorry. He's gone – and I can't reach you.'

Gerry half sat up again; again David signalled him back. But his movement woke Massey who was now bolt upright, staring at them, his eyes searching their faces, a look of incredulity on his own. 'What?'

'You've been dreaming,' said Gerry. 'You were calling out our dads' names.'

That expression of vulnerability was still on Tom Massey's face. 'What else?'

'You were trying to get to them,' said David. 'But you couldn't. You said, "He's gone. He's gone and I can't reach you."'

'Yes.' There was sweat on his brow and his hands were shaking.

'Who's "he"?' asked Gerry.

'I don't know. My festering imagination, I suppose.' He forced a laugh.

'Martinez?' persisted David.

'He wasn't involved,' Massey said wearily. 'I've told you that. Your fathers had an accident. Don't you believe me?' He was speaking fast, his words running into each other.

Gerry shot a warning glance at David. They had to leave him alone now, with such a gruelling day's journey in front of them.

'I've just realized something,' muttered Tom Massey.

'What is it?' David clutched at the hope of a revelation.

'I haven't taken any photographs for *Geographica* yet.'

8

As they packed up the tent, Gerry and David found themselves deeply affected by the bleakness of the valley and mountain in front of them. From the plateau they could see black volcanic rock, partially covered in a glacier running down into a valley that looked as if it had been forged in hell. It was broad and shallow and had enormous pressure ridges running across it, rather like dunes in a desert except that some were splintered and fractured. Black boulders grew out of these, forbidding monoliths that looked as if they were the totem poles of some once-great civilization. The silence was like a wall while the ice glowed blue under a steadily climbing sun – a golden orb in a cobalt sky. Maybe somebody has cursed this place, thought David – made the valley timeless, ageless, caught in its own warp, turning the travellers who dared to cross its frontier into these dreadful, polished monoliths.

Beyond the valley rose a range of mountains with the dull white of their glaciers beginning to become translucent with the rays of the sun. As opposed to the valley, they looked welcoming, promising a safe haven, although David was sure that this was not going to be the case.

'What's up?' asked Gerry, while Massey checked that nothing had been left behind and took some photographs.

'I'm just being daft,' replied David, ashamed at another display of weakness.

'What is it?'

'That valley – it looks horrible. Kind of bewitched.'

'I know what you mean, but there's something else – something much worse.'

'Massey?'

'Haven't you noticed? He keeps sweating and shaking.'

'Do you think he's got a fever?'

'I think he's cracking up.'

With their skis on their backs, the heavy snowshoes on their feet and the damp feeling that would later become insulated warmth, David and Gerry felt at least a little more experienced to face the rigours of the Antarctic landscape. They had plastered anti-glare cream over their faces and lips and they wore the goggles that would hopefully prevent snow-blindness.

Tom Massey, uncharacteristically silent and preoccupied, led them into the valley below.

He looked distracted and wary, continuously glancing from left to right. Gerry and David put it down to the possible presence of Martinez.

The wind in the valley was slight and erratic and seemed to come from any direction. After a couple of hours, having reached an outcrop of ice-covered rock, they rested, eating a Mars Bar each and drinking a little water. Even in the valley, the glare from the snow was tremendous, and when Gerry took off his goggles it was so bright that he hastily replaced them. Occasionally Massey took a nip from a flask and they began to feel even more concerned. Was he drinking alcohol? If so, how could he possibly justify drinking in such hazardous circumstances? wondered Gerry. Had he been drinking early that morning? Did that account for his strange mood?

'It's just as Shackleton said,' said Massey suddenly; it was almost as if he was speaking to himself.

'What is?' David asked him, trying to get Massey to meet his eyes. But it was no use. Massey simply gazed out across the glistening snow to the mountains beyond.

'It is as though we were truly at the world's end and we were bursting in on the birthplace of the clouds and the resting place of the four winds. We're being watched with a jealous eye by the forces of nature.'

'That's exactly what I've been thinking ever since we got here,' replied David eagerly, trying to re-establish some intimacy between them all. Gerry nodded in agreement but Massey ignored them, staring silently into the distance, and David felt a surge of panic. It was as if he had forgotten their existence.

Now they were moving on again, beginning to climb, using their ice picks as they slowly traversed the glacier. This one was steeper and much harder going but the picks held and their boots didn't slip. As they climbed higher they found that the ice was wind-eroded into ridges which made the going even harder as some of the ridges had overhangs, producing miniature chasms.

'I think we'll get roped up,' said Massey in a sudden but reassuring return to normality. 'You could break an ankle here and I know the way across.'

Once roped, they were forced to travel at Massey's pace. Worse still, he seemed quite detached again, moving so fast that they were breathless in seconds. Gerry eventually yelled, 'Stop!'

Massey looked round in surprise and they could both see a blank look in his eyes. Was he on the edge of some kind of breakdown? Had the blow to his head last night affected him, or was he simply drinking steadily and suicidally from the flask. The idea of being in the company of a drunk in such a situation was impossible to cope with. But then David felt a burst of reassurance. Whatever Massey was doing, he would never endanger them.

'What's up?' Massey asked.

'You're going too fast.'

'Sorry.'

'Are you OK?' asked David.

'Yes. Why?'

'We thought you looked a bit – spaced out.'

'It's just that Steve's death is getting to me. I keep thinking of him lying back there. On his own.'

Immediately they both felt callous and insensitive.

'Want a rest?'

'We're OK,' replied Gerry. 'Just slow up a bit.'

They continued to traverse, the ice and snow sparkling in the brilliant sunshine.

Then, without any warning, Massey began to fall.

His ice axe flashed past David who was on the end of the rope. Seconds later, Massey rolled past him, hands and boots flailing for a hold on the ridges but failing every time to get a grip. Gerry was dragged down with him, also trying to get some kind of hold, but Massey's bulk made it impossible. Then David felt the deadly sharp pull of the rope. For a lunatic moment he thought he might

113

be able to support their combined weight, but with whiplash cruelty he was jerked off the ice and began to roll painfully from ridge to ridge. Above him, the bland blue emptiness of the sky mocked their audacious attempts at even presuming to battle the Antarctic.

The fall seemed to go on for ever, and time after time David glimpsed the sombre valley below with its monolith rocks that now looked like tombstones. He hit his head on an ice ridge, grazing his wrist on another. This is it, he thought. This is the end of it all and it is going to be horribly painful. He began to sob hoarsely as they all three continued to tumble down the glacier until, with a shuddering jolt, he found himself on a ledge, spread-eagled across Gerry with Massey dangling across an abyss.

Their combined weight on the rope had brought him to a halt, but Gerry, who was lying on his front, could see Massey swaying over the chasm. A wrong move now would take them all toppling down. Once they had started rolling they had careered across the glacier, ending up in this appalling predicament.

'Don't move!' yelled Gerry. 'Don't move a bloody inch.' I knew this would happen, he kept thinking over and over again. I knew it.

'I'm being pulled,' shouted David.

'You're not.'

'I am!'

'Grab something or we'll go over the edge!' Gerry screamed at him.

'I can't.'

'There *must* be something.'

David eventually managed to lock one of his snowboots under an ice-covered rock and a gloved hand clung precariously to a lip of the ridge.

'I've got some kind of grip.'

'Hold on then.'

'What are we going to do?'

'I can see him. He's about four metres down, hanging out in space.'

'Is he conscious?'

'He's not saying anything.' Gerry yelled down, 'Are you OK, Tom?'

There was no reply.

'Tom!'

Still no reply.

'Tom!'

'Yeah – don't move.' The voice was thin and unsteady.

'Can you climb up?'

'For Christ's sake stay put while I try and get back on the face.'

His voice sounded steadier but desperate, and they both heard Massey grunting and gasping as he tried to make contact with the ice-covered rock. His efforts seemed to continue for an eternity while the pressure on their entwined bodies became more unbearable with each swing.

Gerry desperately sought for better handholds, but his legs were pinned down by David. He was more than halfway over the edge himself and could not only see the twenty-metre drop but the black pinnacles of rock below, encased in shiny blue ice. They were like knives. He could also see that Tom Massey's efforts were becoming increasingly weak. If they all fell, they would be skewered like kebabs by the shards below.

'Try for that arched rock. Just above you,' shouted Gerry.

'Can't . . . reach . . . it.' Massey's breath was coming in great strangled gasps.

'Try again.'

'Can't—' Massey made another attempt but his swing was considerably reduced.

'You've got to keep trying.'

'I can't.'

'Tom—' Gerry had slipped into the role of a cross between a coach and a cheerleader, but watching Massey's attempts was making him sick and dizzy.

Then he felt David moving and immediately began to slide helplessly forward.

'For Christ's sake – what are you doing?'

'Trying to get a grip.'

'You'll have me over. Idiot!'

'Sorry.'

'Stay the hell where you are.'

'OK.'

They were both wheezing now and their heavy, panicky breathing seemed incredibly loud.

Massey began to try again, gasping piteously at each attempt, and Gerry knew that he was using up every ounce of his strength. He had to go on encouraging him.

'You were almost there with that swing.'

'No.'

'Yes. Try again.'

'I can't.' Massey's voice was so weak and despairing that Gerry could barely hear him.

'You must.'

'No point. No strength.'

'Think of Steve.'

'Dead.' He was hanging like a puppet and Gerry had the weird feeling that he was the puppet-master. If he was going to save the situation, he must find the right strings. Pulling the wrong ones could make the little marionette below him kill them all. What was more, he felt himself sliding; only fractionally, but he was definitely sliding.

'David?'

'What?'

'You're slipping . . . I'm slipping.'

'No.'

'Bear your weight down.'

'I am.'

'More, you bastard.'

'I am, you bloody idiot.'

They continued to swear at each other, but with a great effort on David's part their fractional descent was corrected, only the dead weight of Massey like a ball and chain round their bodies.

Panting, gasping, his heart pounding, close to tears now, Gerry tried again. 'Tom, think of Steve.'

'Dead.'

'Think of Martinez. He killed him. You're going to get him.'

'No.'

'You're going to get him, Tom, and you're not going to let us die.'

'Can't move.'

'Yes, you can. I'm going to count up to three. Then you go for that rock – with everything you've got. Do you understand?'

'I'll try.'

'Try hard. I'll count.'

'Wait.' Massey's voice was so quiet, Gerry could only just hear him.

'What for?'

'Just to gather – some strength.'

'It's all in the mind,' called Gerry. 'You know it's all in the mind. Now try.'

'OK.'

'One. Two – and three.'

With an incredible effort, Massey swung, launching himself at the arched rock with a wild cry. His gloved hand caught the edge and, for a second or so, he clung on. Then he lost his grip.

'Try again.'

'It's no good.'

'It is!'

'I'm finished.'

'If you are, so are we.' Gerry gave an appalling cry of despair that David would always remember. 'We're slipping again.'

And indeed they were.

David regained his grip on the rock almost immediately, but the experience was enough to reduce Gerry to tears of rage and frustration and abject fear.

'You'll kill us all!' he screamed.

'I can't hang on all the time.'

'You've got to. Can't you do anything properly? You're just a ponce—'

'You're the ponce—'

'Shut up! Just shut up or I'll bloody kill you.' Gerry was beside himself with rage.

'You won't get the chance – we're going to—'

'Shut up – and keep that grip.' His rage made Gerry supremely authoritative. 'Do exactly what I say.'

'OK.' David pulled himself together. 'OK – I'll hang on.'

'Make sure you do. Tom!' Gerry bellowed down. 'Tom!'

There was no reply.

'Tom?'

Still no reply. Massey was just swinging gently to and fro. Could he have passed out?

'Tom! You've got to speak to me.'

Eventually a weak reply came back. 'Yes?'

'We'll have one more try!' Gerry was fierce. 'I'm going to count.'

'OK.'

'Give it everything you've got. For us all.'

'I'll try.' His voice was very faint.

'One. Two. Three.'

Massey swung, connected – and lost contact.

Gerry cried out in shared pain and bitter, bitter disappointment, and David knew that was it. Massey couldn't go on any longer. Already he could feel the deadly tug of the rope. It was just a matter of time now.

Massey swung again.

This time he connected with the rock and his grip held while Gerry closed his eyes against the misery of it all – and then opened them again to see that, miraculously, Massey was still there. He was clinging on, and he looked secure.

Gradually he began to inch his way into a crevice of the ice-covered rock, ramming his crampons into the scant hold and clamping his arm into the angle of the arch. Then he swung himself further on into safety, and although there was a terrifying jerk on the rope, it then slackened off again.

'He's done it. He's bloody done it,' wept Gerry.

David howled with triumph. 'What's he doing now?'

'Climbing. Climbing like a monkey.'

In fact, Tom Massey was climbing more like a geriatric ape, but Gerry was determined to be wildly optimistic and kept shouting encouragement while David, lying across Gerry's legs with his limbs wedged in ice and rock, did the same, blindly, desperately, the tension giving him adrenalin.

'Go for it, Tom. Get up there!'

Occasionally Massey paused as he clambered on to the top of the arch and the rope grew taut again, but eventually he was slowly climbing towards the top and to the easier handholds that existed in the bare rock which had not been so much exposed to the elements. As he climbed, Massey seemed to grow stronger, more confident, more technically assured.

Then he slipped again – and with a terrible cry scrabbled, caught, scrabbled again and then fell.

The rope paid out, pulling Gerry even nearer to the edge.

'Hold me!' he yelled back at David.

'I can't.'

'Hold me!'

'I'll lose my grip.'

But Gerry held, caught by a small outcrop. It must be rock, he thought desperately, not just ice. Please, God, let it be rock.

Meanwhile, Tom Massey dangled below them, in the same position as he had been before, just like a rag doll.

He'll never do it now, thought David. Never. He'll have lost what little strength he had left.

For some time, the doll figure was completely stationary. Then it began to swing again, slowly at first but soon with increasing momentum.

'What's happening?'

'He's trying again,' exclaimed Gerry. 'He's trying again – and he's going to bloody make it. He's a genius.' He began to yell into the chasm, his voice bouncing off the rock and giving a curious, dull echo. 'You're going to make it, Tom. You're going to make it.'

Gradually, the swing began to widen until Tom was brushing – and then grabbing – at the rock. This time he clung to it for a while, gathered all his last remaining strength and then pulled himself up into the arch with a yell that mingled pain with triumph. Gerry and David cheered as he began to climb. He was out of sight now and it was like listening to a radio play, made weird and surreal by the dull thud of their voices.

'What do you reckon he's doing?'

'He's coming up the rock. The rope's going slack.'

'Take it easy, Tom,' yelled David. 'Take a rest.'

Massey seemed to take his advice, for several times he paused and they could no longer hear the crunch of his boots on the rock. Then the rope went taut and they thought he had slipped again, but soon they knew he was climbing slowly, steadily, with greater and greater assurance.

'He's coming up!' yelled Gerry.

'Be careful, Tom,' shouted David. 'Please be careful.'

He was, and a few minutes later Massey had hauled himself up to the ledge beside them.

9

Massey's breathing was stentorian, so loud and rasping that Gerry and David thought he was going to have a coronary, but at last it grew easier and he lay on his back, drinking in the cold, pure air as if he was a fish out of water, still making a horrible wheezing sound. Slowly, he began to detach the rope and scrambled off Gerry's legs, but Gerry took some time in moving because he had cramp. When the circulation had returned he crawled over to join David, who was already kneeling by Massey's side, gazing down at him as if he was worshipping someone miraculous.

After about a quarter of an hour, Massey's breathing became less ragged and he tried to croak something out.

'Don't try and talk.' David gave him some water which Massey swallowed slowly and painfully.

'I've got to—'

'Drink,' said Gerry commandingly. 'Drink slowly.'

*　　*　　*

More time passed as Tom Massey slowly recovered from his ordeal. 'You saved my life – both of you,' he said at length, painfully struggling into a sitting position.

'No,' said Gerry. 'You were incredible.'

Massey shook his head impatiently. 'You saved me. You gave me the will to live.' His breath reeked of alcohol but neither Gerry nor David said anything.

Massey was right; they *had* saved his life. Modesty and self-effacement had no place out here in this frozen wilderness. There had to be a greater sense of reality, a certainty, a truth; it was the only way anyone could survive.

'I – I want to talk to you.'

'Yes?'

'I've got something to tell you.'

Gerry glanced across at David, squatting down beside him. 'What is it?'

'I – I wanted to—' Then the light faded in Tom Massey's eyes. 'I really trust you now,' he said, speaking hoarsely and quickly. 'You've proved yourselves. We're all equal.' He ended in almost a gabble. 'And you saved my life.'

Gerry and David were both quite sure that this was not what Massey had set out to tell them, but what else could he have been trying to say?

*   *   *

Slowly, shakily, Massey got to his feet, checking his equipment and finding that even his skis had survived their encounter with the rock-face.

'Will we make the base by tonight?' asked David.

'If we push it.'

'But can *you* push it?'

'Yes. I'm just glad to be alive. That'll give me the motivation to get there. We *could* camp out the night but there's always the danger of Martinez, and we've got enough physical dangers out here to keep us on our toes. I'm sure you'll agree with that.' He paused. 'Do you think you can hack it over that mountain?'

'We can hack it,' said Gerry.

'And what's more,' David added, 'we're going to look after *you*.'

To their amazement, tears welled up in Tom Massey's eyes and he turned away. For a few moments they watched him struggling to control himself. 'So it's back to the glacier then,' he said at length. 'I know you won't like it, but we do need to be roped together. Again.'

They nodded, nervous of the idea but seeing the sense behind it. Sore, bruised and shaken, the trio roped up again and slowly began to inch up the glacier. David felt they were bonded together spiritually now and he felt a sense of soaring elation. He had never pitted himself against the elements before and he was beginning to realize that now he was more alive than he had ever been in his life. There was also the joy – the absolute joy – of being close to his father. At last.

Painfully, they traversed the glacier and, with relief, clambered out on to virgin snow again. The going was easier now, but more dangerous, for a maze of crevasses opened up, difficult to see in the dull white light, some of them extremely deep and a few thinly bridged with snow. Others had a thicker covering but these were even more deceptive and Massey was continuously on the alert.

Towards the early afternoon, despite his goggles, Gerry began to see double and then his vision became so blurred that he could hardly see at all. For some time he said nothing, putting the condition down to fatigue, but when Massey announced they were going to have to cross a crevasse on what he said was a particularly thin snow bridge, he came clean.

'You've got snow-blindness,' said Massey decisively.

'What's that?' asked Gerry despairingly.

'The blood vessels in the eyes swell up – that's why you've got such poor vision. Don't you feel you've got sand under your lids?'

'Something like that.'

'OK. I think I can fix it. Have you been taking your goggles off?'

'A bit. They were getting really tight and uncomfortable.'

Massey pulled off his rucksack and began to rummage about inside. 'Don't take them off again, however bad they feel. What I'm going to do is to drop some cocaine into both eyes and then put in some sulphate of zinc. I've never found anything better. If you don't do something about it pronto, the eyes begin to close up – and then it'll be the blind leading the blind.' He laughed at his tiny joke and began to apply his primitive treatment.

Although the substances stung, Gerry's eyes soon began to clear and his vision returned to normal.

'Thanks.'

'We have to rely on each other out here.' Massey put back his own goggles. 'It's good, isn't it? To be mutually reliant. You saved my life – I can heal your eyes.' He spoke so sincerely and in such an unaffected way that David and Gerry were deeply moved. They both felt very close to him now and another rush of elation filled David. This really was sharing and caring, and for the first time in this frozen wilderness he felt optimistic. Companionship was great, he thought. He had never experienced anything like it – and would probably never do so again. David turned eagerly to Gerry and saw the same light, the same knowledge in his eyes.

'Now for the crevasse,' said Massey.

They walked on a few metres and paused, their optimism and elation modifying. The bridge was a thin strip of ice and snow. Underneath, a wide crevasse plunged down into glinting darkness.

'Will it take our weight?' asked David.

'It did with your fathers.'

'That was ages ago. Maybe it's melted a bit since then.' Gerry was obviously worried.

'It looks stronger if anything,' said Massey stoically.

'Can't we go round?'

'If we do, we'll put hours on the journey. We've got to risk this.'

Gerry still looked uneasy but said nothing, and David guessed that although he didn't fancy the slim bridge and the vast drop, he didn't want to say so.

'Are you both OK?'

They nodded.

'I advise you to simply walk straight over without stopping. Don't on any account look down. I'll go first. If I lengthen the rope I can get to the other side without you two following behind me. You only come over when I've got there and I've secured myself against the rock. Then, if anyone falls, or even if you both fall, you'll be on the secured rope and not on each other like we were when I went down the glacier. Do you understand?'

Again they nodded.

'OK.'

We're completely in his hands now, thought Gerry. Their positions had been reversed.

Once Massey had adjusted the rope, he began to walk slowly but confidently over the all too delicate-looking bridge. Gerry and David watched him go, amazed by his courage considering what had happened earlier. He had certainly recovered not only his nerve but also his authority, and they both admired his resilience.

'I'm shit scared,' said Gerry.

'Vertigo?'

'Yeah.'

'But you were staring down at Tom swinging around in that chasm,' said David. 'Did you feel bad then? Because if you did, you certainly didn't show it.'

'I felt pretty sick and dizzy but I was lying flat, wasn't I? It's standing up that does it to me – all that increased height.'

'It's not that much of an increase.'

'It is to me. Up here – in my mind.'

David knew that Gerry was telling the truth about his psychological make-up and wondered if he should alert Massey. But what could he do? He'd already taken every possible precaution.

David looked at his watch. It was 2 p.m. The sun seemed to have lost its warmth and the sky was full of scudding, patchy cloud. Did this mean another change in the mercurial Antarctic weather? He wondered what the elements had in store for them, and felt afraid. The hostility of the landscape was now far more of a threat than Martinez.

'Go first,' said David. 'Get it over with.'

'You sure you—'

'Go on!'

'OK.' Gerry was clearly reluctant. He began to walk to the edge of the bridge, stopped and then, after what seemed an age, took his first slightly faltering step. With rising anxiety, David watched his slow progress. Of course Gerry was quite safe on the rope which David could dimly see was attached to a large, jagged lump of black volcanic rock. *Should* he warn Massey? But what if he disturbed Gerry? He'd better keep quiet. Then he noticed that Gerry's slow progress had practically come to a halt. He was inching forward, a little shuffling step at a time. Then the steps stopped.

Gerry had been determined not to look down but his gaze had been drawn as if by a magnet, and when he saw the wide crevasse below him he was gripped by a blind panic, his brain sending out incoherent signals that turned his legs to jelly and reduced his stomach to a trembling mass. There were snakes inside him, crawling everywhere.

'What's up?' asked Massey gently.

'Nothing.'

'Come on then – I've got some Mars Bars here.'

'Yes.' He was still stationary.

'Don't you want one?'

'Yes.'

'Then move!'

'Yes.' But Gerry didn't move. The cold seemed to permeate his body, making him shake so hard that he couldn't control any of his limbs. He went down on his hands and knees, looking into the darkness of the crevasse, thinking about his father, knowing he might join him, feeling the deadly, deadly cold that knifed into him to such an extent that he wanted to scream – and go on screaming.

'Get up.' Massey's voice was less gentle.

Gerry said nothing.

'Get up!'

'I can't.'

'You must.'

'I want to crawl.'

'You're not *doing* anything.'

'I don't *want* to do anything.' Gerry now had the voice of a young child, torn between a tantrum and a sulk. Inside, he could hear himself silently screaming and he was surprised that the other two were not remarking on it.

'Get up.'

'No.'

'Move on then.'

'No.'

'Don't be a fool, Gerry. You can't stay there for ever.'

'I don't like it.'

'Move!' The gentleness was gone, replaced by sharp command.

'I'm going out to him, Tom,' said David.

'He may grab you.'

'You said the rope could take the weight of both of us.'

'Let me go on trying.' Massey was firm. 'Now come on. Move your arse.'

But Gerry didn't move at all.

'Move!' Massey's voice was hoarse, but nothing could shift Gerry. He seemed to have gone into a trance, crouched on the snow bridge, staring ahead and not moving a muscle.

'Let me try,' pleaded David.

'OK – but remember what I said. Don't let him grab you. The rope will definitely hold both of you, but it'll swing like crazy. And in this case it'll bash you against the sides of the crevasse, and that won't be pleasant.'

David was quite sure that it wouldn't be. Neverthless, he began to move little by little over the bridge until he was about half a metre away from Gerry.

'If you stand up I'll grab you round the waist,' David said to Gerry as naturally as he could.

'No.'

'Then we can go across together.'

'No.'

'You can't stay here. We've got to get to the base.'

'We're going to die.'

'We've *got* to get to the base,' repeated David, while Massey watched them both intently. 'We've got to.'

'No.'

'Don't be such a bloody fool.'

'We're going to die,' Gerry repeated in a monotone.

'We're not.' David moved nearer.

'Careful,' said Massey softly. 'Just be careful.'

He touched Gerry on his rigid shoulder. 'Stand up – and don't say no again.'

Gerry didn't move.

'Please.'

Still he didn't move.

'For your dad's sake. He doesn't want you to die.'

'I want to go to him.'

'He wants you alive.' David was firm. He could see that Gerry was no longer rigid but trembling all over. Was this a good sign or a bad one? He didn't have time to find out.

Gerry slowly rose to his feet. 'Hold me,' he said.

David took him round the waist, but the trembling had now turned to a violent shaking – a shaking that threatened to plunge them both into the abyss.

'Steady. You've got to get a grip on yourself. Stop shaking.'

'Can't help it.'

'You must. I've got you. Just walk towards Tom.' But David was all too well aware that the tone of his voice was far from confident.

'I can't.'

'You've *got* to try.'

David glanced across at Massey, who gave him a thumbs-up sign.

Gerry's teeth were literally chattering now and David was amazed to see the phenomenon actually taking place. The irrelevant thought crossed his mind that maybe Gerry's hair would stand on end soon. But it didn't.

'Start walking.'

Without warning, Gerry started to move and David was so surprised that he almost slipped. With remarkably quick reactions he got himself together, wrapped his arms around Gerry's thin waist and they moved forward like a pantomime horse.

'Well done.' Now it was Massey's turn to talk them down, and it seemed incredible to David that the roles had been reversed so quickly.

But Gerry was not there yet, and as they neared the other side he went rigid again.

'What's up?'

'I can hear Dad,' he whispered again. 'He's talking in my head.'

'What about?'

'He's asking how Mum is.'

'Keep moving.'

Gerry inched silently on. Then he said, 'He wants to see me. Dad wants to see me. He's down there.' He came to a complete halt and glanced down, letting out a little whinny of fear. 'If I jump down, he'll be waiting for me. Won't he?'

'Move, Gerry!' yelled David. 'You've got to get to the other side.'

'Come on, Gerry,' encouraged Massey. 'You were doing really well. Don't stop now.'

'I can hear him calling,' Gerry repeated. But then he began to move. After a while he said in a much more normal voice, 'I thought that was your department, David, not mine. You're the one who hears voices.'

'Come on, you two!' yelled Massey. 'What are you doing out there? Having a committee meeting?'

When they were both safely off the bridge, Massey said, 'Well done, both of you.' David saw the warmth in his eyes and the joyful relief.

'I'm sorry.' Gerry was back to his old practical self, shamefaced and embarrassed. 'I felt so weird out there.'

'That's what this place does to you,' said Massey quietly. 'It can drive you mad, and it happens to the best of us.' He grinned disarmingly. 'Let's have those Mars Bars and a brew-up. Then we'll have to push on – if you're both up to it. Unless you want to take a longer break?'

'No,' said Gerry. 'I want to move on.'

But the next few hours contained the worst physical hardship that either David or Gerry had ever encountered as they climbed away from the slippery rigours of the glacier and on to the impacted snow and ice of the granite mountainside. Although there was more grip, the climb was slow and incredibly tough. They were still roped together, and although Massey was sensitive to their exhaustion he still pushed the pace hard, stopping every hour for chocolate and once for a brew-up of coffee. The breaks became goals, the food and drink so delicious that they were all heady with delight, but the slow, spreading comfort disappeared all too quickly as they pitted their wits against the slopes again.

As they neared the summit, the snow underfoot became soft and they often plummeted up to their knees and sometimes up to their waists. This made the going even worse and the deadly chill of the deep cold began to penetrate every part of their bodies. David and Gerry became numb, only their fingers and toes aching with the pain.

Gradually, as they descended the other side, the snow ran out and they were struggling down black volcanic rock which was gritty and smelt acrid. For some reason, David was reminded of brimstone. Could this be what brimstone smelt like? When they looked down they could see a rolling valley which was covered with another long glacier stretching from the mountains to the seashore. A range of mountains rose darkly to the east.

'Keep going that way and you'll arrive at the South Pole. Eventually.' Massey grinned but even he looked grey with fatigue. 'But there's Rothera. You can just see it on the promontory.'

The tiny toy buildings gave them a feeling of comfort and relief.

'Where's the Argentine base?' asked Gerry.

'Up the coast. You can't see it.'

'You don't think he's waiting for us?'

'I'm going to double-check first. When we get down there I want you to wait at the diesel store – that's a few hundred metres away. Then I'll come back to collect you.'

'What about the memorial?' asked David anxiously.

'I thought we'd build the cairn down by the sea tomorrow morning before we set out for the rendezvous, and maybe do a bit of wood-carving. Then we can photograph our handiwork. My wife used to be a wood-carver – it was her profession.' He paused, brewing up more coffee on the primus in the shelter of an overhang. His hands were shaking again but David and Gerry put that down to the bitter cold. Gerry could have wept with the pain in his hands and feet and David felt much the same. The thin blue flame of the primus didn't seem to have any power, but eventually it did produce three mugs of reasonably warm coffee.

Clasping his hands round the precious heat, Gerry said, 'I didn't know you had a wife.'

'I don't now,' said Massey. His voice had no expression. 'We split up a long time ago. She didn't like wet Wales – or me,' he added with surprising candour.

Gerry and David realized that he wanted to talk and, despite the freezing conditions and the now cold coffee, they felt they had to let him go ahead.

'It would have been nice to have had some kids,' said Tom Massey reflectively. 'That was why I was so fond of Steve, I suppose. I mean, he was one hell of a handful but I did see him – see him as a son.' His voice trembled slightly. 'It's terrible to think of it, but you know how it feels – you lost your fathers. That's a fact I'm not likely to forget and it must have been terrible coping.'

But the point is, he's got to cope with the loss of Steve, David thought. Shouldn't I be giving more to Massey? Sharing something specially private with him?

But as usual Gerry got there first.

'When I lost Dad, I almost lost my mother too. We were all so much part of each other. I suppose that's the problem with only children – just by chance neither of us has any brothers or sisters.'

'Is it by chance, though?' said David. 'Our fathers were so busy charging round the globe that they only just had the time to have us as far as I can see. That's why my mother walked out. I've been brought up by my aunt. Dad was hardly ever at home.'

'And you resented that?' asked Massey.

'I got used to it.' He looked down at the desolate landscape. Somehow it seemed right to have this conversation here rather than round a cosy fire.

There had been ice in his heart for a long time and now it was all around him. 'I loved him, though. At least – I loved the idea of him. I can hear him calling to me all the time – in my dreams, that is.' He glanced at Massey and was shocked to see the pain in his eyes. Hastily he asked him, 'What were Steve's parents like?'

'I never met them. He was in community homes from the age of two.'

'But they exist?'

'Somewhere.'

'Didn't he ever want to meet them?' asked Gerry curiously.

'I think he was afraid. I suppose he didn't want to run the risk of being rejected again.'

'Did you get close to Steve?'

'Too close.'

'What do you mean?' asked David.

'He got to know me too well.'

'Does that matter?'

'I'm not a good person to know so well,' Massey rapped out and quickly turned to Gerry. 'How is your mum getting on?'

'I don't think she can bear to live without him.'

Again, David saw the pain in Massey's eyes. 'But she'll – she'll come to terms with it eventually. I'm sure of that.'

'I hope so.'

'Have *you*?'

'In one way. I feel he's part of me – locked away inside. But coming out here – I love the place. Just like he did. That's helped.'

Massey nodded, looking pleased in an almost childish way, but David couldn't agree. So far they had eluded the traps this deadly place had sprung, but only so far.

'When is the *Patriot* putting in?' he asked.

'We've got a slight problem,' said Massey. 'A problem I only discovered half an hour ago when I checked out the radio. I thought we'd push on a bit before I told you, so that you could have a reassuring sight of the base.'

'What's gone wrong?' asked David. The trap was sprung again.

'It's not a disaster,' Massey hastened to reassure them. 'But when I was trying to get back up the rock after that fall, I must have bashed the radio so hard that I've damaged it, and it won't function. I've checked it out several times.' He held out the battered two-way radio for their inspection and they could both see that one side had been completely crushed. 'But Captain Devon knows he has to rendezvous at three each day and he'll keep to that, I promise you.'

'There's no way of repairing it?' asked Gerry.

Massey shook his head but passed Gerry the damaged radio. Taking a look, Gerry passed it back. 'I see what you mean.'

'Exactly. But it's not something to worry about. Directly we meet up with the ship, I'll go with the helicopter pilot and pick up Steve, and the Captain will send off a shore party to try and locate Martinez. I reckon he's at the Argentine base, but from a diplomatic point of view there could be a few problems. However, I'm sure the British authorities will sort him out.'

'It'll take time,' said Gerry.

'Yes, you may be back in England a little late, but at least you'll be on board the *Patriot* and you'll be safe.' He paused. 'I don't suppose you've felt like that with me.' There was an unsure note in his voice.

'You've been terrific,' said David.

'And really looked out for us,' added Gerry.

'Yes. Well.' Massey sounded as if he couldn't stand talking about it any more. 'I reckon we could ski some of the descent. What do you think? It's not all ice.'

He was right. There was a broad sweep of snow on the other side of the glacier.

'What about crevasses?' asked Gerry.

'It's solid.' Massey sounded totally confident. 'I've been down here before.'

The skiing down the long slope to the valley was not only exciting but incredibly beautiful, with the virgin snow crisply zipping around their blades and the frosty early-evening air suddenly making even David think he was travelling through Jack Frost's kingdom. He hadn't thought about the magical land his mother had told him about in years – not since he had been a very young child – but the words came back to him as his skis whooshed down the valley with the snow flurries like a wake behind him.

A great happiness surged inside Gerry and with tremendous exhilaration he followed Tom Massey down the slope which was already beginning to flatten out as they neared the coast. His optimism surged. Despite the radio, they were going to be all right. They would soon be warm and dry, and eating hugely. Then there would be the joy of building the cairn and eventually boarding the *Patriot*.

Once on the flat, ice-ridged plain, they took off their skis and began to tramp towards the base.

'I'm knackered,' said Gerry, and David suddenly realized how utterly exhausted he was. Wave after wave of fatigue swept over him, reducing his legs to lead and his stride to a stumble.

'Nearly there now,' said Massey comfortingly.

They weren't, but after another hour he was able to point out a long, low building that he said was the diesel store and, beyond that, the building that was Rothera Base. Twilight had fallen at last and a crescent moon sharply etched the weird ice sculptures that had been created by wind and blizzard, rearing up out of the ground like sentinels.

They arrived three-quarters of an hour later and crouched down in the lee of the store's roof which was overhung with icicles.

'I shan't be long – say twenty minutes at the outside. I want to check the whole place out.' Massey looked as exhausted as they were. 'Brew up some coffee and have something to eat. Try to keep yourselves warm.'

As he spoke, they heard a distant rumbling that grew steadily louder and louder. Then there was a huge bang – and silence.

'He's shooting at us,' yelled Gerry.

Massey grinned.

'What's funny?' rapped David irritably.

'Sorry. That's only part of a glacier breaking off into the sea to end up as an iceberg.'

'I thought it was Martinez.' Gerry was ashamed.

'Not a chance.' He grinned at them. 'I'm off. Back soon.'

He strode away, leaving them gloomily contemplating the primus. They had made fools of themselves – reduced themselves to kids again, just after being on an equal level with him. Looking thoroughly annoyed, Gerry busied himself with the stove but David didn't join him. Now that Massey had gone he felt lonely and uneasy.

10

As Gerry brewed up coffee a sharp little wind blew in off the sea, stirring the snow and making them feel even more intensely cold than before. We're so near but so far, thought David. He felt dispirited and saw that Gerry was now staring out towards the ice-ringed sea with its dead white bergs. He looked equally despondent.

'We'll be in the warm soon,' David said, trying to cheer him up and to counter the anticlimax.

'Yeah.'

'It won't take Massey long to check out the base. It's only small.'

'Do you think the weather's changing again?'

'Shouldn't think so,' David replied without the slightest knowledge either way.

'I think it is.'

'Massey will be on his way back soon.' Suddenly David found Gerry deeply irritating. Why was he never positive? Never *ever* optimistic.

'I wouldn't count on that.'

'Why?' asked David, becoming angry, but only

147

out of utter exhaustion. What was he on about now?

'Well – he's not exactly efficient, is he?'

'Massey? He's been great.'

'Has he?' asked Gerry sourly. 'Losing Steve? Falling about in chasms? Trying ice bridges when they're dangerous?' He paused. 'I mean, his track record's not very good, is it – even if you ignore what happened last year.'

'Do you think there *is* any chance of finding their bodies? Just so they could be buried properly?' David was trying to change the subject but also to give an airing to the flimsiest of his hopes.

The remark seemed to sting Gerry's pessimism into open contempt. 'How can you say that?'

'Say what?'

'They'll be under a few hundred metres of snow and ice, wherever they are.'

'There might be a chance,' said David vaguely.

'There's no chance.' Gerry was shouting now, his rage mounting. He felt a great proximity to his father out here but since Massey had gone on his reconnaissance, he had seen Steve's corpse again and again in his mind. But it bore his father's head. 'Anyone would know there's no chance – anyone but an idiot like you.'

'What's up, Gerry?' David tried to be reasonable, to diffuse their argument, but his own anger was mounting again.

'It's you. You're such a prat.'

'Thanks.'

'And Massey's an irresponsible idiot.'

'And you're so bloody wonderful? You couldn't even tackle that bridge, could you?' David tried to stop himself saying the hurtful words but his rage – still born out of cold and exhaustion – drove him on. 'The only reason you're criticizing me and Tom is that you're ashamed of being chicken, like Steve was.'

'Rubbish!' Gerry clenched his fists.

'Bloody true.'

'Want me to sort you out?'

'Here?'

'What's wrong with here?' Gerry came nearer, fists upraised.

'I'll take you on any time.' David, who hadn't had a fight in years, was stung into action. He'd beat the living daylights out of the bastard.

'Come on then,' said Gerry.

They stood watching each other. In Gerry's eyes, David saw something hostile and primitive like the ice, and all his rage disappeared, replaced by a feeling of revulsion. Almost at the same time, Gerry unclenched his fists and put his hands behind his back. 'Your eyes,' he muttered.

'What?' demanded David.

'I could almost see chips of ice in them. It's being out here. In this awful place. Do you think our fathers felt that same blinding, meaningless rage? Do you think they killed each other?'

'Don't be ridiculous.' David was scoffing. 'They were great friends.'

'So were we.'

'We still are.'

'We almost weren't.'

'We've *got* to be on our guard – watch out for the times when we're at a low ebb. Like now.'

They brewed up more coffee and continued their vigil, each with the conviction that they would remain friends for the rest of their lives. They had stood aside from the violence they had wanted to inflict on each other, and both knew that because of this they had passed the ultimate test.

'Where the hell is he?' said Gerry when half an hour had dragged past.

'Still checking.' David tried to be resolute.

'It's only a glorified hut.'

'Maybe he saw something.'

'Maybe Martinez topped him.' Gerry grinned to take the edge off the comment. 'I'm freezing.'

'You would be. This is the South Pole,' said David and laughed, trying to drain away the spreading apprehension.

'Let's go and check him out,' said Gerry.

'He said to stay here.'

'For half an hour?'

'If we move, we might miss each other,' said David doubtfully.

'How can we? The ground's flat.'

'There's all that weathered ice.'

'We still can't miss each other,' Gerry reasoned, but David knew that he was waiting for his decision.

'OK. Let's go together.'

Cautiously they approached the base, which was composed of a prefabricated metal cabin and a flagpole with an idly moving Union Jack. The wind had dropped but occasionally it re-emerged in little spurts and the flag began to flap unpredictably, taking them by surprise. They continued to move forward slowly, trepidatious now, wanting only to find Massey and to be reassured that this sombre adventure was coming to a close.

Then, without warning, a large bird seemed to come from nowhere, flying low over their heads and emitting an unearthly screech. They could both feel the movement of its wings as the bird soared away from them.

'What the hell was that?'

'Skua,' said Gerry. 'Must have been disturbed.'

'Mad, you mean,' muttered David, trying to make a joke but failing completely.

Now they were beside the door of the cabin. There was still no sign of Massey.

'It'll be locked,' said David.

'Let's try.' Gerry pushed hard and the door swung open noiselessly.

'What's going on?' whispered David. The interior was dark and the crescent moon gave them no light at all. They listened intently but could only hear the waves sighing on the ice.

'Is there a light?'

'There must be a switch.' Gerry stepped inside and felt around the wall. 'No luck,' he whispered, trying the other side.

'Wait a minute.' David's voice sounded unnaturally loud in the stillness. 'We're complete idiots. The generator won't be switched on, will it?'

The interior was painfully cold.

'There'll be kerosene lamps,' said Gerry hopefully.

'And calor gas – except that we don't have any matches.'

'We'll find some.' Gerry was determined not to be defeated, moving cautiously around the hut and eventually finding a torch on a side table. After a minute or so of fumbling, he managed to flood the interior with its powerful beam.

The arc of light swept the walls and they saw that the building was composed of one central room with half a dozen bunks squeezed into a corner, a small laboratory in the other while the remaining walls held bookshelves, charts, photographs of polar explorations and a small, partly sectioned-off kitchen with a couple of store cupboards. In the centre of the room was an open fireplace and a steel chimney, around which were grouped chairs and a table. Beside the table was an oil drum.

'That's odd,' said Gerry. 'There's a trail of snow leading up to that thing. That proves Massey's been in here at least.'

'Or someone has,' muttered David.

They hurried over to the rusty oil drum and saw in the torchlight that a metal lid was placed insecurely over the top.

'We'd better see what's inside,' said Gerry, stepping back so the arc of light widened. 'Get it open.'

David pulled at the lid, which was partly stuck as if it had been hurriedly rammed home with some force. It took him a few seconds to prise it open. Eventually he managed to pull it up and the metal disc clattered to the floor. He stared inside unbelievingly. Slowly, instinctively reluctant, Gerry joined him.

Steve was encased in ice. He looked up at them glassily, the wound on his chest blue and frosted. David stepped back with a little whimper while

Gerry gazed down at the familiar face in disbelief.

'Martinez,' David whispered.

'Why?'

'I don't know. How the hell do I know?'

'But how?'

'What do you mean, how?'

'How did he get him here?' Gerry persisted. Despite the shock he wanted to cling to some logical explanation.

'By helicopter?' David was too horrified to think straight.

'We'd have seen it,' scoffed Gerry.

'By boat?'

'What boat?'

'The *Zenith*?' asked David uncertainly. 'Which way did Massey say Martinez was going?'

'Can't remember. Anyway, he'd have had his own boat – why use ours?'

'Not if he'd come overland.'

David was determined to be logical. 'Listen – he could have picked up Steve, put him on a sledge or something, and taken him back to the dinghy.'

'But why?' Gerry searched for a reason.

'I don't know. The whole business sounds crazy,' said David. He didn't want to search for theoretical explanations. He just wanted to make things happen. 'Let's go down to the beach and find out.'

*   *   *

Gerry shone the torch over the uneven blocks of ice and rubble as they hurried down to the crackling sea. 'Here she is.'

There was no doubt that it was their Zenith lashed to a rock, bumping around in the shallows. Inside the dinghy was a sledge.

'He's around here somewhere,' said Gerry. 'Must be.'

David could hardly contain his desperation now. 'Where the hell *is* Massey?'

The *Zenith* continued to bob up and down innocently, the ice creaking and groaning around it.

Suddenly, with shattering intensity, there came a blunted roar which was so primeval, so utterly alien that David's heart began to pound, the pain making him gasp out loud.

Gerry, meanwhile, was peering out into the semi-darkness, his eyes searching for the source of the dreadful sound. It was repeated again and again, but the silence that followed was far worse than the discordant, barbaric cry. The sweat gathered clammily under their polar suits as David also stared out into the freezing Antarctic twilight. Maybe there was some creature out there no-one had discovered – a creature that lived under the ice and snow.

'What is it?' whispered Gerry. 'What could it be?'

But David had no answer.

11

The moon came out from behind a cloud, giving jaundiced light to a beach littered with stranded icebergs, sculpted into bizarre shapes. The massive skeleton of a whale lay on the pebbles, the network of polished bone making an almost melodic sound as the wind filtered through it. The bestial cry came again and again until Gerry suddenly punched the air with relief. 'I know what that is. It's an elephant seal. There's a whole colony of them over there.'

'Won't they attack?' asked David, his nerves in shreds. He could see them now, about a dozen bulbous fleshy mounds floundering on the tide-line, watery bloodshot eyes staring threateningly as they approached. For a moment he wondered if these creatures had eaten Massey alive and the next clean-picked skeleton would be his.

'No, their pups are almost full grown. They should be fine.'

David shuddered as they passed the largest elephant seal. Its huge body and blubbery face made it obscene-looking, the resemblance to an elephant all too clear. With huge snouts and blunt, tombstone teeth, they were nightmare creatures on their dawn-of-time beach.

'The big one is the beachmaster,' whispered Gerry. 'The winner of all the fights against the other bulls. They're designed for a life at sea – they only land to breed and moult. But it's strange to find them – they're usually on sub-Antarctic beaches like South Georgia. Maybe a storm pushed them up this far.'

They stopped to observe the seals, forgetting they were increasingly feeling the cold and that Massey's protracted absence was becoming unbearable. They found the seals a temporary respite, a distraction from the grim realization that they were soon to uncover more horrors.

'That trunk thing,' David said. 'It's so repulsive.'

'It's called an inflatable proboscis.'

'Yuk!'

'You shouldn't be so squeamish. It's only an enlargement of the nasal cavity.'

David wrinkled up his nose in disgust. The things made him feel sick.

'The cavity normally hangs down over the mouth, but it can be erected to form a kind of cushion,' Gerry persisted. 'It also acts as a sounding chamber to amplify the roar.'

'You mean belch?'

'Roar,' said Gerry firmly. David felt a rush of affection for him. Only Gerry could take an interest in an elephant seal's nose at a time like this. He wished he had known Gerry's father. Like his son he had undoubtedly been an odd-ball, far more interested in the natural world than the human one.

'There's something behind the beachmaster.'

'Just another seal.'

'It doesn't look like a seal. What's more, it can speak. Can't you hear it calling?'

The sound did resemble a human cry, but David wasn't convinced.

'I don't know what we're on about, watching these seals. We're running out of time and—'

'That could be Massey. Come on!' said Gerry abruptly and began to run down the beach, giving the large elephant seal a wide berth. It roared at him as he ran past its rancid, seaweed-hung hulk.

The man was dragging himself up the snow and ice-covered pebbles, moving so slowly that his progress was barely discernible. He wore a tattered polar suit with the hood half off, revealing fair hair and a long pale face. One side of his suit was badly slashed, and they could both see a wound over which blood had congealed.

'Are you Martinez?' asked Gerry.

He stared back at them uncomprehendingly.

'Martinez. Argentine geologist,' repeated Gerry impatiently.

'Martinez?'

'Who *are* you then?' asked David.

'Sven Lombost. Swedish geologist.' The man's voice was very weak and he kept glancing around him as if he was expecting pursuit.

'What's happened?' Gerry knelt down beside him.

'He tried to kill me – I knew he might. That's why I brought murdered boy.'

'*Who* tried to kill you?'

'Massey.'

Gerry and David stared down at him in disbelief, but Lombost continued: 'He murdered boy. Almost got me too. Knife wound. You have to help.'

Gerry wondered just what game this man was playing. No doubt he was an associate of Martinez and it was all some kind of set-up. He looked around the desolate beach, wondering where the other man was hiding.

David was thinking much the same. But where *was* Tom Massey? They certainly couldn't manage much longer without him.

Lombost began to cough.

'We'll get you into the base,' said Gerry. He sounded sharply efficient, uninterested in the lies that were no doubt going to pour out as glibly as Steve's.

David put the dilemma into angry words. 'Where's Massey? What have you done with him?' He glanced at the rocks at the end of the beach. Could he be lying out there injured?

'Cave.'

'Which cave?'

'Minerals. I met him at cave. My company promised him big money if he could show minerals.'

'And did he?'

'Yes. I wanted check him. When you land I follow – see killing.' Lombost began to cough again but David was determined to capitalize on his injury. Once under shelter, he would be in a better bargaining position; out here, he *had* to tell the truth. Eventually.

'We're not helping you until you tell us what's *really* going on,' said David. 'Isn't that right, Gerry?'

He nodded. 'You'd better give us the truth and stop lying. Now.'

'I'm telling you truth,' said Lombost. He tried to sit up and failed, turning on his back, his eyes filling with tears of pain. 'Massey said the deal was so secret that I had to come alone from Jarcon Sound – that's some miles away.'

'Do you mean your deal with Massey was illegal?' asked Gerry.

Sven nodded. 'I had to see cave. Confirm mineral deposit. Put body on sledge and then in *Zenith*. I got the boy in hut and put him in drum.' He paused, tried to gather some strength, and continued. 'Massey made radio contact and said he would be late. He was, but I waited in Argentine base up the coast and made journeys down here. He eventually showed up and said he didn't have much time – that things had gone wrong. He wanted to meet me later but I insisted we went to cave, said that I'd put the money there but only I knew where it was hidden. As soon as he showed me where minerals are I intended to alert Argentines, show them the body, get them to arrest him. But Massey demanded money at once. I said I hadn't got it. He threatened me but I hit him hard and thought he was unconscious. I made it back to the beach but he followed with knife. You came and he went back.'

'Why are you lying to us?' demanded Gerry.

'I have to get in warm. I can't—'

'Where *is* this cave?' said David angrily.

'Over there. Behind rocks.'

'Why hasn't the cave been discovered before?' asked Gerry contemptuously, obviously not believing a word of Lombost's story. They both stared down at him, listening to his ragged breathing, and David felt a twinge of guilt. Suppose they pushed him too far? Suppose he died on them? How serious was his injury? The questions jostled for priority in his mind, but he was still completely sure that Lombost was lying. There could be no doubt about that.

'*Edmund Watson* – old ice-breaker. Driven ashore maybe to conceal entrance. You've *got* to get me help.'

'Is there anything else we should know?' asked David relentlessly.

'Your fathers. He killed them.'

'No,' said David. 'You or Martinez did that.'

'You are stupid. You believe Massey.'

'Of course we believe him.' Gerry was totally confident.

'This Martinez—'

'Yes?'

'He doesn't exist. Massey must have made him up. To keep you feeling threatened. To provide reason for boy's death.'

'Listen – keep your lies to yourself,' said David. 'How do we get to this cave?'

'Behind rocks. You'll see the wreck.'

Gerry bent over and looked more carefully at Lombost's wound. 'I don't think this is deep.'

'I assure you it's not self-inflicted.' Lombost was clearly in great pain. 'You must not go to cave. Massey will kill you. You have to get to Argentine base. Get help. You mustn't look for Massey. You promise me,' he gabbled at them feverishly and then closed his eyes. 'Please.'

Between them, David and Gerry carried him back to Rothera Base where they laid him on a bunk, lit the kerosene lamps and made a fire from the already stacked driftwood.

Lombost's eyes had closed again but he was breathing more regularly. Gerry, who knew fractionally more about first-aid than David, had carefully cut away some of the blood-soaked clothing to reveal a long, ragged gash across the Swede's stomach. Although he had lost a good deal of blood it wasn't, as Gerry had suspected, particularly deep. He tore up a sheet, found some antiseptic and crudely but firmly bandaged him up as best he could. Then he and David moved over to another part of the room, shivering in the intense cold away from the fire.

'He's obviously protecting Martinez who's presumably holding Massey,' said Gerry.

'Shouldn't we get help?'

'The Argentines are a mile up the coast. Anything could happen while we're away. Maybe it already has. But we've got to try and get to him.'

David nodded, not wanting to chicken out but determined to try to weigh up the odds. What was the point of them being captured too? Or worse. 'There could be more of them around—'

'Sure, but we'll never make the Argentine base in time. We've *got* to get to him now.' Gerry remembered Massey's commanding voice on the snow bridge and David felt again the exhilaration, the bonding, the joy of physical companionship.

Massey had done so much for them. Now it was their turn. 'Let's go,' he said.

Gerry returned to Lombost who was staring up at the ceiling, clearly trying to summon up the strength to argue with them again. 'When we get back I'll try and clean up that wound. The *Patriot* will be here tomorrow.'

'You mustn't go—' Lombost was in considerable distress. 'Massey's dangerous. He'll—'

Gerry tucked the blanket more tightly round Lombost, while David built up the fire. 'Rest,' he said quietly. 'That's all you can do.'

But Lombost tried one more time. 'You stay here. Barricade door and wait for ship.' He gazed feverishly at them. 'He'll kill you – like he killed your fathers. How can you be such fools? Why won't you believe me? Then he'll come for me. Understand?'

The wreck of the old ice-breaker was covered in ice and starkly lit by the moon. Almost broken in two, she was stranded on the beach and they could just make out the name *Watson* on her eaten-away bows. Small bergs were clustered around her stern and they emitted a low growling as the sea buffeted them.

'Maybe they discovered the mineral belt first,' said Gerry. 'And the crew of the *Watson* mutinied. Ran her ashore to hide the cave.'

'They made a pretty good job of it.' Certainly there was no sign of even the slightest hollow or indentation.

'More likely they were trying to excavate the minerals and she got washed up on to a lee shore.'

'You'd think her owners would have salvaged her.'

'Here? No chance.'

The cliff was black and fortress-like, with a few glaciers running down its eroded face. With all his recent experience of the Antarctic, David had never seen such a formidable place. It was like the ramparts of hell.

'How do we get across?' Gerry was scanning the rock-face. There was a slight fluttering movement and he realized that hundreds of birds were nesting in the crannies.

'Through the ship. If we can get up to her top deck we'd have a chance of checking out the face. Why the hell didn't we get more accurate instructions from Lombost?'

'Because we were up to here with his lies.' Gerry was angry and impatient. 'He wouldn't have told us anything.'

They cautiously walked up the broken gangway that led into the dark heart of the *Edmund Watson*. Dim moonlight filtered the devastated and derelict interior, a skeletal network of rusting and barnacle-covered bulkheads, ladders with most of their rungs missing and decks that had half rotted away under the weight of ice and snow. It was also ominously clear that the sea regularly invaded the ship, and as they clambered up to the top deck David had the nightmare vision that at any moment they would be drowned by an ice-cold tide.

'Stop!' Gerry whispered hoarsely, and David felt sick with fear.

The elephant seals lay in a stinking cluster, the snouts and teeth and deep-set eyes pointed in their direction. Suddenly Gerry relaxed. 'They're dead,' he said. 'They must have come in on a high tide and couldn't get out again.'

The threat of the sea reasserted itself as they climbed another broken ladder, skinning their hands on the flaking iron and taking giant steps because of the missing rungs, until they arrived shivering on the top deck, wishing they hadn't made so much noise.

The sea was stirring below them and the breeze was becoming a lashing wind, bringing the wreck to life in a cacophony of rattling metal.

The blackness of the cliff was broken by glaciers and it seemed impregnable. Then Gerry spotted another ladder.

This time it was far less corroded, probably having been dragged from somewhere in the interior of the ship. It led down to a narrow ledge which was partially masked by a mass of snow-covered rock and about twenty metres above sea level. When they looked up they could see a narrow gap in the cliff.

'Could be a way in,' said Gerry, 'but we'd never climb that – it's sheer. There must be another entrance.'

'Keep your voice down,' hissed David. 'They're probably holding him prisoner in there.' An image of Massey as a captive filled his mind as well as the realization of how fond he had become of the man. If only he could have shared as much with his father. That's what Massey had become to him over the last few days. A father figure who he had grown to trust – and to love.

'There's nothing here.' Gerry battled with his vertigo as they inched along the ledge. 'It's all rock and snow.'

'Move on a bit,' whispered David, wondering when Gerry's fear of heights was going to tell.

'It's just – wait—'

'What is it?'

'There *is* a gap – it's small but we can probably squeeze through. It may not go anywhere though.' Gerry began to push his way into the fissure.

'Watch out there isn't a drop the other side.'

'No – there's – there's a shelf of rock. Quite wide, but the torch doesn't show up much.'

David followed Gerry into the tight, dark space and after a lot of manoeuvring found himself on what he sincerely hoped *was* a ledge. 'Hang on,' he whispered. 'This side seems to slope down.' He flashed the torch, but the beam only showed a dark descent. 'And I can smell something.' Seaweed, he wondered. Would they be going below sea level? That seemed a particularly unpleasant idea.

The rocky ground fell away below them and it was just possible to climb down, feeling their way, occasionally flashing the torch, trying not to slip on the greasy surface. The descent seemed to go on for ever, the roof getting lower until they were both half-crouching, trying to subdue acute claustrophobia. Just when it was becoming unbearable there was suddenly more height and they found themselves standing almost upright again.

There was total silence. Were they in some kind of cavern? How high was the roof? Could they risk scanning with the torch? There was a slight dripping, stirring noise. Could that be water? But there was a crunching sound, too.

Slowly they both became sure that what they were hearing was floating ice, nudging, grinding.

12

'I think we're at the bottom of a very narrow crevasse.'

'A crevasse?' David asked disbelievingly.

'Look up.'

Very faintly, he could see light – just a grey glimmer and nothing more.

'There's ice on the rock-face – can't you see it shining?'

'Wait. I thought I heard something.'

They listened for what seemed a very long time until they heard a slight wheeze, but it was mixed up with the slow sighing of water and the movement of the ice and was therefore hard to identify. Then they heard it again.

'That *is* someone,' said Gerry.

'Or it's the wind. Hang on. What's this?' David picked the object up. 'It's another flashlight.'

'Does it work? whispered Gerry, his nerves screaming.

'I can't find the switch.'

'Give it to me.'

David handed the flashlight over.

'Come on!' he said, unable to bear the wait.

'For God's sake,' snapped Gerry, 'just shut up, will you?'

'You're meant to be mechanically minded—'

'I am.' The beam snapped on, and Gerry began to play the light on the rock.

He had been right. They were standing at the bottom of a very narrow crevasse carved out of granite. High above them, on one side, a glacier snaked down, narrowing the gap and almost obscuring what little light there was from the moon. The cavern fell back from the crevasse and was huge, with cathedral-like proportions, and on the far side there was a lake of black ice.

'Are we at sea level?' asked David.

'Just about, I should think. Maybe the tide comes in under all that ice.' Gerry played the beam around the surface. 'It's not that thick anyway – or at least it doesn't seem to be.'

The lake fed back into what looked like a smaller cavern.

'Do you think this is where the minerals are?'

'Could be. That wheezing sound—' Gerry was getting rattled. 'What the hell can it be? It sounds human.'

They strained their ears and thought they caught the wheeze a couple of times, but it was difficult to be sure.

* * *

Massey walked out of the inner cavern into the beam, limping slightly, his face twisted in pain. In one hand he carried a knife. His sudden appearance was an immense shock but was also a considerable relief.

'Tom—' David took a step towards him. 'Are you alone? Where's Martinez?'

The silence lengthened, and then Massey smiled. It was a strange smile, sad and reflective.

'I think there's been a misunderstanding,' he said.

'What misunderstanding?' asked David, and heard his voice rebounding from the cold black walls.

'I think you'd better know the truth. I expect Lombost told you about this place.'

'Yes,' replied Gerry quite calmly. 'He told us a pack of lies. Thank God you're safe, but where *is* Martinez?'

'He never existed,' replied Massey, his kind eyes fixed on them intently. 'I'm sorry. I never wanted it to end this way.'

13

'I don't think that's funny,' said David. He didn't understand what was happening. Massey was different. Steve's voice in his head said, 'Someone else comes into his mind and slams the door.' But Steve was a liar just like Lombost.

'I'm afraid I haven't told you the truth, which is a pity because I liked you both.' Massey spoke slowly and carefully as if he was weighing up each word. 'I liked your dads, too. But they had to die – and you have to die. *And* Lombost.' He spoke easily, reasonably, as if murder was the most natural thing in the world.

He's not saying this, thought Gerry. This is one of David's fantasies – his dreams. It's all a joke – he's just winding us up. 'OK.' Gerry tried to laugh it off. 'Stop fooling us. You're hurt, aren't you?'

'Yes. Lombost nearly did for me.'

'So where *is* Martinez?' persisted David.

Massey moved another step toward them. 'I'd hoped to clear up this business and leave you two well out of it. In fact, I'd made the most careful plans but unfortunately they went awry.

What with Steve and Sven, and then the delays. You never can rely on the human element, can you? It always lets you down in the end. But I haven't forgotten that I owe you both my life and that makes what I have to do very hard indeed.'

This is the most lunatic conversation I've ever participated in, thought David. Massey must be suffering from concussion. Then David remembered him drinking from his hip flask. That was it – Massey was cracking up. He'd already had a breakdown and was obviously in a bad state again. That explained everything.

But meanwhile, a deadly realization was creeping into Gerry's mind. There was something particularly logical in what Massey was saying. 'Lombost has radioed the *Patriot*,' he said quickly.

'He hasn't got a radio,' said Massey quietly. 'I took it off him.'

'He must have had another one—' Gerry began to panic.

'Come on!' David yelled. 'What *is* all this?'

Massey looked down at the ice. He spoke slowly, evenly, without the slightest expression. 'Your fathers went through that ice and the tide would have taken them out.'

David stared down unbelievingly at the black lake, but Gerry made a little choking sound.

'The ice is thin because of the tide. I'd hoped to have disposed of Lombost that way, but I'll deal with him later. In the meantime you can join your fathers. It's something you've been wanting to do for a long time, isn't it?'

The rage rose in Gerry's throat like bile, preventing him from saying a word.

'You're hurt,' said David with a slight stammer. 'Why don't you just chuck that knife away, pack it in and come back to Rothera Base with us?' He wasn't going to believe this. He *knew* that Massey was suffering from concussion, or having another breakdown.

'You bastard.' Gerry's anger was like a wasp sting, hard and bright and sharp.

'Gerry,' David pleaded. 'You know he's joking.'

'Don't be a fool,' said Gerry. 'He's rotten through and through. We believed him. We didn't heed any of Steve's warnings. We thought Sven Lombost was lying. But you're the liar, aren't you, Massey? You callous murdering bastard.'

Massey didn't reply, but David could see a bleak, cold look in his eyes that he had never seen before and the appalling truth began to dawn on him. Massey didn't care for anyone; he was a psychopath. David thought of the father he had loved so dearly but had never known. Massey had taken him away for ever, taken away something inside David, taken away— With a cry of rage, he threw himself at Massey, moving so quickly that Massey was taken completely off-guard as

David rugby-tackled him to the ground, the knife clattering away into the darkness. In the light of the beam, they rolled over and over, David's hands around Massey's throat, Massey kicking and punching until they were sliding towards the dark ice of the glistening underground lake. There was a sharp crack as they both hit the surface.

Massey disappeared into the water and David lay spreadeagled on a narrow strip of unbroken ice. The speed of what had happened was incredible, but Gerry's reactions were fast and he lay on the frozen ground, reaching out towards David.

The ice groaned; even if David didn't drown, any contact with the freezing water would surely kill him at once. 'It's still holding,' Gerry yelled. 'But not for much longer. Roll over towards me. Fast!'

David did as he was told and the thin ice below him exploded into fragments. He was now on a slightly thicker wedge nearer the shore and Gerry wondered fleetingly if the water beneath could be shallow, but he was sure it wasn't and as he hesitated he heard the ice beginning to split. Locking his ankles round a rock, Gerry was able to reach out a few more centimetres, but it still wasn't enough to grab David's outstretched hand. Why couldn't he get closer? Then he saw the panic in David's eyes. He wasn't moving because he was terrified.

'Dave – you've got to reach me. It's only a few centimetres.'

'I can't.' David seemed to have completely given up, and although Gerry had put the flashlight on the ground beside him it only illuminated a tiny section of the ice. He could just see one of David's hands, flat on the ice, and Gerry noticed small details like a cut on one finger, a broken nail on another. He knew that if he allowed David to be swallowed up, he would always see that hand.

'You've got seconds. Move!'

The ice cracked again.

'Move!'

'I *can't*'.

'You must. Remember the ice bridge. How you helped me. Now I'm helping *you*. You've got to *move!*'

'I can't!'

There was more cracking and splintering and Gerry could see the water bubbling up around David's ankles.

'Move!' Gerry screamed at him with all his lung-power. Bloody well move your arse!'

David rolled over a couple of times to the harsh sound of grinding, breaking ice, and Gerry grabbed his wrist. With a final heave he was able to pull David on to the safety of the rocky floor as a widening hole opened up behind him. Dark, freezing water bubbled up and then, through the gap, came Tom Massey.

*   *   *

As David lay beside him, Gerry gazed in bewildered horror at Massey's face. He had actually managed to survive the deadly cold. But for how long?

'Help me.' Massey's voice was thick, forced out through his raw, freezing lips. 'Help me.'

'Go to hell.'

Gerry picked up the flashlight and concentrated the beam on Massey's face. He was hanging on to a piece of ice with taut, blue fingers, but hardly had any grip at all and it could only be seconds before he disappeared.

'Help me. Please, Gerry.'

'You killed my father.'

'Please—'

Gerry ground his snowboot into Massey's fingers, but still he hung on.

'You've *got* to help him.' David was on his feet now.

'No way.'

'We've got to.'

David tried to push Gerry aside but he was too exhausted. Slowly, Massey's tenuous grip slackened.

'You can't let him go.' David struggled with Gerry ineffectively, but Gerry not only managed to hold him off with one hand but also to shine the flashlight into Massey's eyes.

'Drown, you bastard.'

'Please—' Massey's voice was thin now – a ghost of a sound.

'You killed my father,' Gerry repeated.

Massey slipped under the surface, only his hands upraised in supplication.

'We can reach him.' David finally shoved Gerry aside with renewed strength. He grabbed one of Massey's wrists and yelled, 'You take one and I'll take the other.'

But it took them a long time to drag Massey out on to the harder ice, and even longer to pull him on to the floor of the crevasse. By this time their hands were numb and they were breathing in loud, harsh gasps.

David lay on his back, his whole body trembling with cold and exhaustion. 'How is he?'

Gerry didn't reply.

'How is he?' David staggered slowly to his feet again.

Gerry was crouched beside Massey.

'What's the matter?'

'He's gone.'

'No—'

'It was the cold.'

'But we got him out.'

'Too late.' Gerry's voice was wooden.

'Let me take a look.' David knelt down. Massey was still, his face blue, his eyes wide and staring.

Nevertheless, David tried mouth-to-mouth re-suscitation but after a while realized there was nothing he could do for Massey.

'I let him die,' said Gerry.

'No.'

Gerry turned angrily to David. 'Don't lie to me. I need the truth. Right now I really need the truth.'

'It was understandable—' David began.

'Understandable? An eye for an eye? A tooth for a tooth? Who the hell do you think I am?' He paused. 'Who the hell *am* I? Another Massey?'

'How could you be?'

'That's the way it starts.'

'He killed your dad – and—'

'Does that give me the right to kill *him*? Don't be a fool.' Gerry shook his head in rising anger but there was a kind of disbelief too – a disbelief in himself. 'Face the truth. I killed him.'

'He would have died anyway.'

'That's not the point.'

David knew now that he couldn't – shouldn't – try to gloss over the enormity of Massey's death. He knew that he would have to leave Gerry to his private agony, to come to terms with it himself. All David could do now was talk, make plans, keep them both busy.

'I suggest we leave him here. When the *Patriot* comes, they'll collect him.'

Gerry knelt by Massey's side as if he hadn't

heard. David stood behind him and put his hand on his friend's shoulder. Suddenly he felt old – much older.

'Come on. We've got to go.'

Slowly Gerry rose to his feet and they both gazed up at the moon that cast pale light down the crevasse. Then a brooding malignant shadow rose at the very top. David thought it was a skua.

14

The beachmaster roared as Gerry and David walked slowly up the beach to Rothera Base. A grey, freezing dawn was gradually coming up over the iceberg-littered bay. Another skua hovered above the wreck and then dived over the pebbles, hoping to find something living and helpless and edible.

Once inside Rothera Base they found Lombost in a state of considerable agitation and, for a while, all he could do was to wrap his blanket closer around him and mutter, 'Thank God you're back.' He then asked about Massey, and David gave him an edited version of what had happened.

'It's good,' he said, and David glanced at Gerry and then quickly looked away again. He couldn't bear to see the misery in Gerry's eyes.

'Was there – a bag in the cave?' Lombost eventually asked uneasily.

'Your pay-off?' said Gerry viciously. 'You can get someone to look for it when they take Massey away.'

They stoked up the fire and sat round the flames like animals comforted by the light. Lombost slept and Gerry sat staring into the red heart of the crackling wood. Outside, the wind howled on the frozen beach. David fancied the elements sounded angry and mortified, as if survival was not something they had planned.

After a while they both plunged into deep sleep and were only awoken by the chattering sound of a Chinook helicopter. David and Gerry ran out on to the beach, waving desperately, terrified that the chopper might fly away again, leaving them in this menacing wilderness, but the pilot saw them at once. He slowly began to descend, the helicopter's blades sending the snow scurrying over the frozen beach whilst the elephant seals screamed abuse at the invader. As it landed, great flurries of snow ascended, blotting out the beach and sea almost completely. When the pilot jumped down and ran towards them, ducking under the swirling blades, David imagined for a ghostly moment that his father was running towards him out of a snow storm. He almost called out his name.

'It'll get better,' said Gerry. His voice was shaky.

'At least we came here,' replied David. 'At least we got as close as we could.'

Later, as the *Patriot* appeared on the horizon, they built a cairn on a small promontory overlooking the bay while the Chinook crew brewed tea, cooked food and dressed the gash on Lombost's stomach.

The monument took most of the day and when they had finished, Gerry and David carved their fathers' names on a block of driftwood and lodged it safely halfway up the cairn. It read:

In loving memory of Adam Preston and Peter Bishop who loved this wilderness. Died February 16th, 1993.

Gerry had added a part of one of Shackleton's poems that had been a favourite of his father's. It seemed to have particular relevance to what had happened – even to their relationship with Tom Massey, for David could still remember, with a hollow bitterness, how he had grown to love the man.

And the love of men for each other that was born in
*   that naked land,*
Constant through life's great changes will be held
*   by our little band,*
Though the grip of frost may be cruel, and
*   relentless its icy hand,*
Yet it knit our hearts together in that darkness
*   stern and cold.*

'I hope I've remembered it right,' said Gerry.
'You've forgotten someone,' pointed out David.
They carved another plaque which read:

In loving memory of Steve Beck. Died January 28th, 1994. Age 18.

As David and Gerry walked away from the cairn to watch the *Patriot* anchor out in the bay, they turned to gaze back at their monument. A snow petrel was sitting on the top, puffing its feathers out and seeming to watch them intently. Then it took flight, soaring up to the pale, cold Antarctic sun.

Epilogue

Some months later, David Bishop received a note and a photograph from a British geologist who had been responsible for verifying the mineral seam near Rothera Base.

Dear David,

Whilst climbing inside the crevasse I came across a message which I think your father must have cut into the rock before he died. Using some high-powered lighting equipment I managed to photograph the lettering. I enclose the print.

With kind regards,
Roger Cadagan

The image showed hurriedly hacked wording, carved in the ice face. It read:

DAVID. I LOVE YOU. DAD.

THE END

HELL ON EARTH
by Anthony Masters

CRASH-LANDED IN THE RAIN FOREST!

Alone in the Amazonian rain forest, their plane in flames and the pilot dead, eighteen-year-old Joe and his friend Sam face an almost hopeless situation. Hundreds of kilometres away from anywhere, equipped only with a knife, a compass and a map scrawled by a desperate, dying man, they are to need every ounce of their courage and strength to survive within the great, remote silence of the forest.

And Joe and Sam must face more than the natural dangers of this alien, primitive world. For they have a valuable stone belonging to an Indian tribe – a stone that could save the forest from the ravages of the timber companies. But there are others after the stone – evil, merciless men who are prepared to kill anyone who gets in their way . . .

A gripping adventure, packed with action and authentic detail.

0 553 40522 5

A SELECTION OF ACTION/ADVENTURE TITLES AVAILABLE FROM BANTAM BOOKS